GEM

An American Story

Dennis Hill

LeRue Books an
Imprint of LeRue Press
Reno, Nevada
www.LrpNv.com

Order additional copies :
LeRue Press, LLC
280 Greg Street, Suite 10
Reno, NV 89502.
www.LrpNv.com

Bulk purchases and school discounts available. Contact LeRue Press.

Author's photograph by Margaret Brown

Library of Congress Control Number:2019956384

Published under the LeRue Books imprint by LeRue Press, LLC.
ISBN : 978-1-938814-24-2

10 9 8 7 6 5 4 3 2 1

Dedication

My father did his best to instill his work ethic in me. Eventually his ideas proved true and I came around to his way of thinking. My mother instilled her love of books in me and it took right away. I would like to think I earned an "atta boy" from the two of them.

Acknowledgements

It's common knowledge this kind of work is solitary; it is also common knowledge that it doesn't get done without lots of help. I am lucky to have the help and support of my siblings; things like that ought not to be taken for granted. As usual, my good friends Penny Mazzola, Luke Whalen and Carol Snyder stuck by me and gently suggested when I was in over my head, often. As usual my wife, Margaret, worked her life around things like, "Would you mind stopping whatever it is you are doing and read/listen to this line and tell me your thoughts". Last, but by no means least, Jan, Lenore and Kathleen, the women of LeRue Press. They put it all together and made it happen.

Prologue

In the late summer of 1945 I was somewhere in the Pacific Ocean, I was an electrician's mate second class.

My duty station was the USS Hugh W. Hadley DD774. At this moment there was not a lot going, as a direct result of the battle for Okinawa on 11 May 45. I don't know how many kamikaze's came at us that day, I do know we shot down 25 of the bastards. Our ship was, for all practical purposes, done with the war and we were being towed home. As you might guess, this point did not escape conversation and rumor among those of us still on board. I'm sure the thought of going home or staying in the fight plagued every one of us, as it has all combatants since the beginnings of warfare. One of the truisms of military life is orders and we all had ours. It was not our decision; still, most of us devoted a good bit of time to it. Truth be known, in my case Dec 10 1941 was the day I put my John Hancock on the enlistment papers and I had seen enough death and destruction to last ten lifetimes. All of us would go back if asked, and all of us prayed we would never see those orders.

A week or so into the trip a supply ship tied up alongside and we off loaded our part of the cargo and our mail. In the Navy, mail can get delivered with some degree of regularity. For obvious reasons, this didn't always hold true.

There was a long letter from my mother that started with a mild rebuke, which was clearly deserved, about the lack of communication on the conditions and status of her only son. My sister Kathleen had married a Marine and he had been sent to a Godforsaken place somewhere in the South Pacific with a name she could not spell and no word yet from him either.

She asked had I ever heard of the place and where was it? My sister Kristina had left home and was learning to weld in a shipyard in Oakland. Dad and his cattle market were thriving, and he had some promising colts for me to start when all this madness was over. In a post script at the bottom she told me Maggie Pete had died.

After all of the death and agony of the last four years, a tendency to write it off as just one more, might be accepted, in time, it probably would be. Hell, I had not even thought about Maggie for years. In everybody's life people enter and people leave. For a while in my life I got Maggie Pete and Mr. Richards, for a while. Now it seems they both had left.

Chapter I

1935 Northern California

Despite the depression and over all bad times, my father had done very well in the cattle business. He wasn't high-handed or ruthless; he just understood the ups and downs of the cow market and maybe more importantly, he knew real estate. When he should make a move and when he needed to walk away.

Sometimes when he approached a starved out broke rancher, he would ask if he could lease the place from him and run a few of his own cows. If that was agreeable, he would ask if he would like to stay on and manage the place.

As you can imagine that could be touchy. Most times it did not work out well, sometimes it did. With a few he made the deal read so they had the chance to buy back the ranch. There again, the results were a crap shoot. Like I said, he liked cows and real estate deals but his real passion in life was finely tuned bridle horses. Before he got successful he had the time to make them but now he bought already made ones.

Don't get me wrong here, he loved my mother, my two sisters, and me. Mother always joked if the house was on fire Dad would save the horses, then come rescue us. Could be some truth to that.

He had a 1934 burgundy Cadillac convertible with spoke wheels and great big white wall tires. He drove it all over the west coast to various auction yards and cattle sales. Mother said he should have bought a white one; it wouldn't show the dirt so much. But really, I think she felt it made too big a statement. It was hard times after all.

The auctions were where he would hear about ranches for sale. It was a good day if he could sit on the hard benches of some sale yard and buy a rundown ranch and a good bull or two. In the trunk of his car there was always a well-made saddle, because in his words, you just never know when a guy might get to put a ride on a good horse.

On one of the trips, he bought a pretty good-sized ranch between a little town called Madeline and the even smaller town of Likely, near the foothills of the Warner Mountains.

Don't feel like the Lone Ranger if you never heard of it; not many have. The nearest towns of any size are Susanville or Reno and they are not near.

This is where I come into the story.

School had just let out for the summer, and I had some plans. This was the summer I was turning 15 and the world was my oyster. Like I said I had big plans.

I was wrong about everything. Well not everything. I did turn 15. Sunday dinner was a big deal for my mother. All of us would sit around the table with a meal her and my sisters had spent most of the day preparing and talk about each one's week.

This particular Sunday, my Dad told us about a new ranch he'd bought. Nothing new in that. What was new was he was sending me to it.

"Oh no, Dad; I got plans."

"Oh yes, son; I too have plans."

I told you he was a deal maker. Only thing, I never was part of his deals and now I guess I was.

"I'm sending you and Juaquin to check out the place. I want you to give me your thoughts on the merits of my purchase, gather and brand any and all cattle left on the ranch. There might be a little bunch of horses left; I don't know that. The guy that I bought it from is older than dirt and looks real old timey with a big handle bar mustache. The day I met him he was wearing a shoulder holster with a Colt 1911 sticking out of it. But they say he knows horses and that's really why you are going."

"Is there a vote involved in this?" I asked.

"No, no vote." he replied. "I know you have been spending time with that old typewriter of your mothers. Take it and in your spare time you can write a report for school. *How My Mean Old Man Sent Me Off to Timbuktu for My Summer Vacation.*"

He thought that was pretty funny and laughed. I didn't think it quite so funny and I didn't laugh. My mother jumped in, it wasn't clear to me on whose side.

3

"Every boy should get the chance to know an old man. It's a truly wonderful way to look at the world from the perspective of someone who has looked at the world a lot longer than you."

Little did she know. Little did any of us know.

I made a couple more attempts with my Dad, but the fix was in and northern California loomed large in my horizons.

Actually, after some thought and consideration by the cool and logical mind of a fourteen year old, soon to be fifteen year old brain, this might not be so bad after all.

Chapter II

I had known Juaquin all my life and he was not much of a crack the whip over the boy to make him a man, sort of a guy. Maybe the old guy was some sort of gunslinger. Besides, I really like to cowboy.

I kind of thought my Dad's plan would involve loading us in the Cadillac and we'd cruise east in a leisurely way. All the while taking in the sights and having a little father and son time. Of late it seemed my dad's plan and mine differed greatly and so it came as no surprise my plan was not the actual plan.

The morning we left, my Dad and the Cadillac were nowhere to be seen. Juaquin pulled up in the old Ford V8 stock truck. It was a one ton with dual tires on the back and wood racks for livestock hauling. This particular Ford had a two-speed brownie transmission. That meant on level ground, empty, a fellow could burn up the road at 35 or 40 mph. Only we were not empty.

Loaded in the front part of the rack were two horses. A colt Juaquin was starting that he called Black Magic, even though he was a bay.

Sometimes Juaquin's view of the world was a little different. I was tickled to see the other horse was

Grey Boy, a big nice thoroughbred cross, one of the nicest horses my dad owned. Just behind the horses were three bales of hay, our saddles, tack and our things, packed real nice and neat in two gunny sacks.

In those days it was common for ranch hands to buy a pair of Levi's and wear them all summer or even longer, if it worked out that way. The good ones spent their money on dressing up their horses with good gear and silver. Juaquin was one of those. No matter if it was a good horse or a dink, Juaquin's horses always looked and acted like he was entered into the finals at the county fair.

He was however, not too much inclined to drive and in less than an hour he pulled over and told me he thought it might be a good idea if I drove a while. I had driven on the ranch since I was little, so the mechanics of it were no threat. I hadn't actually driven on the open road. Much less in a truck this size and loaded if not to its maximum, fairly close. Shit, what could go wrong!

Chapter III

Actually, nothing went wrong.

It took about sixteen hours to get there and no Juaquin didn't make me drive all the way. It was dark when we got there. There was no way to know what my new world looked like, until barely three hours later when the sun came up.

There was a pre-arranged place to meet up with Mr. Richards and of course no one was there when we arrived. We fed and watered the horses and left them in the truck for the night.

Juaquin went to sleep by the side of the truck, I stayed in the cab and did the same. To say it was a rude awaking would be an understatement.

Standing on the running board, banging on the window, yelling something at me was an old man with a huge grey moustache that just about covered his chin. My very first thought was, how does this old fella eat?

I came out of that truck like it was on fire. The old guy wasn't much taller than me and in those days I wasn't tall either. He wore brand new Levi's with about a six inch cuff rolled on the bottom. I guess he was like the rest of us in not being able to figure out the Levi shrink.

He was so bowlegged it made his toes turn in. That man was so pigeon toed, I would bet he had a good chance of tripping over the same stick twice.

He wore a suit coat and a vest with a small gold chain attached on one end to the vest and the other to what I assumed a pocket watch. Hanging from the middle of the chain was a small and intricately made replica of a square and compass.

There was no sign of the 1911 Colt my dad had mentioned or any other kind of armament for that matter. It turned out maybe he was a mason, not a gunslinger. He wore an expensive looking straw fedora, the kind you might associate with boulevardiers in the big city, except this hat was framed with sweat marks and stains. It was kinda tipped low over one eye.

He was asking me something, I was so busy looking at him that whatever it was went over my head.

"Who do you think is going to take the National League Pennant?"

"What, who, what?"

"I spent part of my youth in Missouri, so I'm partial to the Cardinals. How about you?"

"I guess I would take the New York Giants, although I've never been to New York."

With that he stuck out his hand. "My name is David Richards, what's yours?"

"Ben, Ben Winters, pleased to meet you Mr. Richards." His hand was hard and calloused, and he about broke my fingers before he let go.

GEM

"You too kid. Now go over and kick your Mexican awake and let's get on down the road to the ranch."

Of course, Juaquin was wide awake and standing off to the side of the truck keeping a sharp eye on things. Mr. Richards had a fairly new Chevy pickup, red, and dented in several places. Watching him drive, the dent's needed no explanation, he couldn't drive for shit.

Juaquin and I fell in behind and away we went, a lot of things going on in my head.

"What do you think of him, Juaquin"?

"I don't know Benny, just one of those old timey kind of guys, he's probably all right. I guess when we see him around horses we will know better."

Typical reaction from Juaquin, his character was defined clearly by his patience. He grew up in Stockton, in a family that could trace its roots back to when the missionaries came to California and Spain still owned the place. How many generations would that be? Who knows?

He grew up with horses and all kinds of livestock. With the exception of going to France and being in the trenches fighting the Huns for a couple of years, horses and cows were all he had ever done. In my view of the world, he had made his bon-a-fides. The part when Mr. Richards said kick your Mexican did not set well with me.

After we pulled off the highway it didn't take but about ten minutes to get to his ranch, well maybe the case could be made (weakly) my ranch. The house was two stories, painted white with green trim around the

9

windows and doors. The windows on the second story fit neatly under the eaves on each end of the house and were bigger than the ones on the ground floor, for ventilation I guess. Over the front door and below the upstairs window was a large front porch that came out maybe ten feet and spanned the whole front of the house. The roof was metal and looked like it had once been painted green, matching the trim. It must have looked pretty shiny in its day, that day being a long time ago.

Mr. Richards was waiting for us in the front yard.

"We started building on this house a couple of years after we got here. There wasn't much money to be had in those days and we would do some more work on it as little chunks of money came in."

"It looks to me like you must have done a fine job, it is still standing." I didn't know what else to say.

"What a battle, the classic case of the blind man leading the deaf and dumb man." Mr. Richards continued. "Several years later when it became available we added electricity. The screened in porch in the back came next and finally indoor plumbing". He kind of pointed east and said, "The barn is down over there. You can unload and put those two horses in the little trap out the back. That's where you will stay".

He turned and walked into the house.

We looked at each other and Juaquin laughed and said, "From the looks of the place he's not as domestic as he once was."

We climbed back in the truck and drove down the lane to the barn. Juaquin's colt could not get off that truck fast enough, Grey Boy just sauntered down the ramp, calm and cool and looked around. As we were going through the barn toward the back, without even looking Juaquin said, "Grey Boy is sore in his shoulders from the truck ride, I can feel it through the lead rope."

"You are so full of crap. You can't feel that."

He smiled and didn't say nothin.

Juaquin was never much of a bullshitter, I guess he could.

There were two pens behind the barn, both good sized. One on each side of the barn door, both had the feed bunks built part way into the barn with dividers set in such a way that ten horses could eat their fill, undisturbed. It was designed so the hay was stored on the upper floor and to feed, all that was required was drop the hay into the feeders. The mechanisms for raising the hay into the loft was also on this end. The water tank was some sort of big tractor tire with concrete for the bottom.

A windmill straddled the tire and the fences were set up so livestock could drink from either pen or out in the pasture on the other side of the fence. The tank was on the far end of the pens and plumbed to automatically keep the tanks full. It was south facing and covered to keep from freezing in the winter. It was plain to see some thought had gone into this part of the building.

Juaquin said, "Pick".

I pointed to the right. "I suppose this one will work until someone tells me it won't".

Juaquin forked down some hay, while I walked to the back of the pen to check on the water. "Full".

Chapter IV

Over the fence as far as the eye could see was sagebrush and big open meadows, this place could run some cows! On the east side toward the back of the barn built under the stairway leading up to the loft was the tack room and it was filled with horse tack, saddles, silver bits, and braided rawhide gear.

In the corner was a bench with leather working tools neatly arraigned on the wall. On the opposite side of the barn was the bunk house, with three metal framed twin beds lined up side by side. A couple of Charley Russell prints were thumb tacked to the wall, along with a pinup of woman in a bathing suit, from maybe the twenties. At the end was a door that opened to the bathroom. On the wall above the sink was a small cracked mirror, a commode, and a shower stall made of sheet metal and water stains. To say it had never been graced with a woman's touch, I guess would be kind.

About the time we got our little camp set up, a woman came busting in all smiles and laughter. She was an Indian, about four foot tall. It seemed she was as wide as she was tall and had the most enormous bosoms I had ever seen. I guess she saw me looking at them, because she put her hands on the sides and pushed the both of em up in my direction.

"Ever see anything like these up close, cowboy?"

"No ma'am".

"Don't worry you won't. That swarthy Latin fellow, you came in with might get a chance. Although I have my doubts. I guess it would depend on the whimsy of the woman." She laughed and I knew neither one of us would ever get a peek at them.

"Yes ma'am."

"I will have food on the table in one half hour, don't be late!"

"Yes ma'am."

Juaquin and I just looked at each other.

"Best not be late."

We weren't. About ten minutes before our time limit had expired, we knocked on the front door and Mr. Richards let us in.

"I guess you met Maggie Pete. She's some punkins that one."

"Yes sir, Mr. Richards we sure did!"

The house was pretty small. The living room and kitchen made up the whole ground floor, that makes it sound bigger than it was. The kitchen took up the larger part and it was neat as a pin, with a huge Majestic wood burning cook stove dominating the room. Dividing the kitchen and living room was what looked like once had been a very fancy and ornate dining room table.

It had seen better days and there was no rhyme nor reason to the chairs around it, they didn't match anything. The remainder of the bottom floor held two blue overstuffed chairs with white crocheted doilies on the arm rests and chair backs. Two floor lamps set on the outside of each chair and between them was a table with a Zenith Stratosphere radio.

The old guy knew his radios, I'll bet it could pick up stations from far and wide. Maybe even those border stations from Mexico that played the swing music, my father thought so little of. On the opposite wall was a book shelf with some pictures on the top.

On the left was a group picture of some soldiers and at the bottom of the picture was written Cuba 1898 in white ink. The next picture was a thin pretty woman with kinda wild lookin hair.

She was wearing dark dungarees with a white shirt and had a pistol strapped around her waist. Her arm was slung gently around the shoulders of a smiling little boy, her other hand was at her side clutching a dark hat with a broad brim. In the back ground behind them was a horse decked out with a silver bit and a two-rein outfit. Next to it were a couple of better horse pictures.

On the far end of the shelf, the last picture, was one of those old-time tin types with two young kids about twelve or thirteen staring out with somber looks on their faces. One of them had on a hat that looked like it had seen some better days. Above the book case, in a richly made cabinet with a glass front, was a sword and its scabbard mounted below it. They both were engraved and as I started over to look what was written Maggie called us to eat. As I sat down to eat it dawned on me there was no way to get to the upstairs.

"Mr. Richards what's upstairs and how do you get there?"

"Bedrooms and to get access go out the back door through the kitchen, the stairs are out there. I couldn't exactly figure out how to put them inside."

He sounded testy. He had been asked this before, would be my guess.

"Besides, it gives us more room in here."

I wondered, was it the blind guy or the deaf one made the decision on the placement of the stairs.

We had scrambled eggs with fried potatoes and it was good. The conversion was lite and pleasant.

Maggie made us all laugh with stories of her no account first husband and how he had run off with a low life, morals of a duck, Pit Indian woman. She told us about having an old woman she knew put a special curse on the lovebirds.

"It must not have been much of a curse, they live just down the highway in Janesville and have enough kids to start a baseball team."

Just to keep the conversation going as we were finishing up, I asked, "Is that picture of the soldier you, Mr. Richards?"

It seemed to get still at the table, Maggie stopped cleaning up.

Mr. Richards didn't say anything for the longest time, then he smiled and said, "No, no that picture is of my son William Clark. He was one of Teddy Roosevelt's God damned rough riders. They buried him in Cuba."

Juaquin who had not said one word during the whole meal, said so soft I could hardly hear the words "He was a hero, sir."

Something passed between those two men at that moment, I would not understand for years. It was the briefest amount of time possible, a blink of an eye, how long does it take for a breath of air or a heartbeat. Two men who may or may not end up friends, had become as close to each other as any human being can. They knew war.

Mr. Richards looked over at me, "Let's go look at your new ranch, Ben."

I didn't know how I should react to that, "sure."

We walked through the barn and Mr. Richards asked me, "If I could whistle Dixie?"

Of course, I could, but was he trying to set me up for some old man humor, was my first thought. "Ya I guess."

"Walk down to the end of the pen. Open the gate by the water tank, whistle Dixie, and walk back up here."

Juaquin kind of smiled at me and shrugged his shoulders.

Oh well, what the hell, let's see what his game is. I did just as he said and by the time I got back up to the barn twenty horses came calmly walking in from the sagebrush. Shit, I didn't even see em in the field.

"Always be polite to horses, my father taught me that, no sense in making it a battle bringing in horses."

The horses lined up in their dividers and waited while Mr. Richards dumped a small pile of grain in front of each horse. However, the old guy turned out. I could see he knew horses!

Chapter V

"Ben, will you ride the bay mare, she is straight up in the bridle. I call her May West, because she has a big chest. Juaquin would you mind putting a ride on that big sorrel gelding, called Heartbeat? He will stand still as a statue while you get on. When you ask him to move out he will take three steps forward, three steps to the left, and then jump three or four times straight in the air, depending on his mood. After that your grandma could ride him all day. Heartbeat. I ride him in 5/8 bosal."

Sure, enough three then three then three.

"He must like you, generally he makes me endure four jumps."

Juaquin was smiling, he liked it when they bucked, a lot.

Mr. Richards put his saddle on a flashy, I mean flashy, yellow gelding about sixteen hands and rode him in the two reins. The horse followed him to an old broke down wagon with one side removed and some cinder blocks stacked up to make stairs. Mr. Richards climbed up the blocks to the back of the wagon and positioned the horse so he could get on, off the wagon.

We set off at a long trot for about an hour, we didn't see any cows. Although the land was flat it felt like we were slightly gaining in elevation. We came to a barb wire fence and Mr. Richards held up his hand, motioning for us to stop. None too soon as far as I was concerned. That old man was tough! The country dropped off from where we stopped, and I could make out what looked like had been a burned out building.

Reading my mind, I guess, he said, "This is the end of the property on the north end. George Williams came to this country around eighteen seventy and prospered, buying up all the ranches and homesteads he could. In those days there were no fences to speak of and everybody ran their cows together. A couple of times a year all the ranchers would congregate around here, gather and see what was what and who belonged to who. I don't have to tell you there were a plethora of cows and cowboys."

The old guy stopped talking and smiled a little.

Was he thinking of an old memory or showin off with plethora?

"Ten years later an old square head named Schmidt built what's left of that building down there and made good money selling cheap whiskey to anybody that had the price of a drink. It took about four days to get everything to the rodear and start the branding. Maybe the moon and stars lined up or some other cosmic event, no one knows. Most of the cowboys and all of the Williams Ranch hay hands thought it might be a good idea to drop by and say howdy to the ol Dutchman and have just one. Not quite two days later the world looked different and all the cows had to be rounded up again.

Right around then George Williams stopped by to check on the progress and saw there was none. He never even got off his horse, just turned around and rode home. The next morning he hitched up a team of mules, tied a saddle horse on behind and he too went to visit the Dutchman. Schmidt came out the door with a big smile and asked what brought the visit.

George smiled right back at him. "I have a deal to propose, I would like to trade this wagon and team for your building."

"No Gott Damned way!" The man was understandably stressed.

Still smiling, "I have a couple of gallons of coal oil in this wagon and I mean to burn down this place whether we make a deal or not. I will give you thirty minutes to get what you want out."

He climbed down and started to unload the coal oil.

That old German didn't say a word, he turned went back inside and got his stuff and thirty-one minutes later that place was on fire. It did not pay to cost George Williams money.

"Man, oh man that was the Wild West." I said.

"I don't know, things just happened, let's head in that direction now." He pointed over his shoulder.

"Sir" We both looked over at Juaquin. "This grass looks real good, where are the cows?"

"They are on the south side. The cows have not been here for going on two years."

"Two years!" It just popped out.

It wasn't a second guess or some sort of a power play from the new ranch representative. It just wasn't the way I thought it was done.

Mr. Richards looked at me like maybe that was the dumbest grouping together of words, he ever heard.

"When the buffalo ran free thousands and thousands would graze a single location, then move on.

When they left the field would look totally decimated and eaten out. It wasn't, what they did was eat it down to a point where new grass could grow. Fertilize it and with their hooves break up the ground, keeping it soft and able to absorb rain water.

But that was not what did the most good, it might be two, three years, maybe more, before they returned. The grass rested."

Once again, he looked at me as if to say, are you smart enough to understand what I just told you?

"Let's get moving and see some more."

If today was any indication Mr. Richards's mode of travel was the long trot, and away we went.

We would stop only long enough for him to explain how a certain water tank was fed and how to shut it off when it was not in use or divert it in a different direction. Sometimes it would be to look at a land mark, we would need to know to find our way home.

Once he asked if we wanted to see the biggest tree in this part of northern California. Not being much of an authority on tree size, to confirm or deny proved impossible. It was a big tree, I'll give him that. The three of us kept the same routine all day. The subject of lunch was never broached.

Once though Mr. Richards did place his horse next to a big rock and used it to get off.

"Anybody need to piss?"

By the time we got back to the ranch, I knew my death was imminent either by exhaustion or hunger. Juaquin asked me if I needed some help with my horse, he seemed no worse for the wear. To say yes would be the wrong answer, I knew that. It was tempting though.

"Maggie will feed us," Mr. Richards pulled out his pocket watch, "At half past the hour." And walked up to the house.

"God Damn, Benny I pray God I will be able to ride a horse like that if and when I get his age!"

At that moment in time, living that long was not a subject I felt much need to ponder.

"How did you do, cowboy? Ride that old man into the ground?"

"No, that was not the case, ma'am."

"I didn't think so." She was so damn cheerful it just made me smile.

"Come on in and sit, supper is ready."

"Ma'am this is a great dinner, thank you." A full belly always brightens a boy's outlook on things.

Maggie smiled in a way that said thank you for the kind gesture. "That old guy is a cowboy tried and true. One time I saw him hit the ground, harder than a blue water sailor knocking on the whore house door."

"Maggie. He is just a boy, he don't need to hear that kind of talk!" The way he said it, I could tell he thought it was as funny as I did.

"Thanks again for dinner, ma'am. Tomorrow is another day, goodnight."

Juaquin and I walked down towards the bunk house.

"That little Indian gal is funny." Juaquin laughed, "I might have to take her up on that offer to check out that chest of hers, up close."

That conjured up a picture in my mind, I'm not sure needed to be there.

Chapter VI

The next morning, I woke up feeling all beat up and tired. I got out of bed, threw a little water on my face, and went out to whistle Dixie.

When the horses came in and lined out in their various places, I gave them their little bite of grain. Mr. Richards and Juaquin came in the barn at about the same time. "Ben, thank you for jingling in the horses, we won't need them today. You and I are going to be drugstore cowboys and take the Chevrolet."

He turned toward Juaquin. "Would you mind capturing that black gelding over there and shoeing him for me?" He looked at Juaquin like he was expecting Juaquin to give him some guff and he was ready for it.

"No sir, I don't mind at all. That sorrel with the white socks, standing three horses down from the black, looks ready too. If it's all right with you, I'll check the rest and act accordingly."

"Ok, thank you. Let's get some breakfast and start our day."

After eating Mr. Richards said, "You drive Ben, I can't seem to really get the hang of it, and don't much enjoy it."

Looking at that truck in all its banged up and dented splendor, I knew he wasn't lying to me.

"Head back down toward the highway, there's a couple of things we need in town before we continue the cooks tour, for your father."

"Sure."

"That Mexican of yours seems alright?"

"That Mexican is alright and he ain't mine, comprende!" The old son of a bitch pissed me off.

"Whoa, whoa climb down from that high horse of yours and accept my apologies, that's not how I intended that to sound. I like Mexicans all right, I once had a crippled Mexican sergeant for my guardian angel."

"Ok, I will. My dad taught me it is ok to get mad, just get over it quick so you can start thinking rational again." Out of the clear blue he said, "I was born in England."

"Didn't you say something about being from Missouri, when we first met?"

"I spent time there when I was young, but I came from England on a ship. My mother died on the voyage and was buried at sea,"

"I'm sorry to hear that."

"Thank you, I was only two years old and I don't recall the slightest detail of my mother or the boat, for that matter. Turn left up here and we will stop at the feed store."

"I see it, there on the right."

He came from England, my mother will get a kick out of that.

He had me back up to the loading dock and we went in the building, it was big and dark, there was a thick layer of dust covering everything. Pretty much like feed stores everywhere.

"Davey Richards, you old skinflint, what are you going to try to beat me out of today?" The voice came from the back somewhere.

"If you watch your pennies they will turn into dollars, I think Benjamin Franklin might have said that."

"You are so full of shit, what would you know about Ben Franklin."

By their tone it was easy to see they had been friends a long time.

"Get out here and meet the newest rancher in the valley."

The owner came out and shook my hand and said, "Meredith Willis owner, operator."

I was a little embarrassed by the new rancher part. However, standing behind him and a little to his side was a girl about my age, with hair the color of straw and pretty blue eyes. I would have liked to shake her hand, but introductions were over, and we walked back out to the loading dock.

On it were ten sacks of grain and fifteen blocks of salt. Mr. Richards kind of motioned toward the stack and the truck, turned around and walked back inside with the owner.

The signal he sent was crystal clear, I started loading the truck. The truck was about half loaded when, the girl walked over towards me and spoke.

"You look young to own a ranch"

"You think it's possible?"

"No."

"You have keen mind for detail, my father is the new owner."

"Rich kid, I take it."

"Well, my father seems to be doing pretty well, I on the other hand don't have two nickels to rub together." She laughed and stuck out her hand, "Jean Willis, you can call me Jeanie everybody else does."

I took her hand it was warm, and her handshake was firm. "Ben is mine". I let go of her hand. "I will call you Jeanie, if you want me too. It seems like it is a fitting name and goes well with an obvious free thinker, such as yourself." Shit, what in the world was all that. That girl isn't going to put up with that sort of hogwash for very long. Embarrassment set in, again.

She turned to leave but didn't walk away instead she walked closer to the back of the truck and lowered her voice. "It's been rumored ol Davey Richards killed a couple of men, out there." She pointed back toward the ranch, "around the turn of the century."

"What?"

Before she got a chance to answer, Mr. Richards came out and said, "Cut the bullshit, boy. We only get so much daylight."

The girl had disappeared back into the dark inside the building and was nowhere to be seen. We got in the truck and turned back on the highway toward the ranch.

Mr. Richards had me drive a short way past the turnoff, until we came to a wire gate. After opening the gate and starting up the dirt road, I started seeing cows and calves. Mr. Richards motioned to stop every once in a while. If there was one, he had me pick up what was left of an old salt block and put it in the back with the new ones.

If you think the inside of a fourteen-year-old boys mind was lit up by what a total stranger told me about a total stranger, that would be a mild way to describe the absolute chaos going on inside my head.

How should I act, what should I say? Davey, old boy, I heard you blew up a couple of malcontents a while back. Mr. Richards could you please describe to me the events that led up to the death of two men of unknown origin? Was there just cause for the use of deadly force or did they simply irritate you? Someone once said discretion is the better part of valor, I agreed with that sentiment and kept my mouth shut.

We slowly moved up the road picking up used salt blocks and Mr. Richards pointing out things and places I should know and remember. Of course, murder was the only thing on my mind. I knew the chances of something like that coming up in casual conversation were remote. I'd let my father sort it out. Maybe some other set of square heads tried to open a bar, this time on Mr. Richards's ranch?

"Ben are you listening to me or are you thinking about Jeanie?"

"Sorry sir, I guess I was." In a roundabout sort of way, I guess.

"Well don't, her mother and dad are very protective of her and besides she is probably a lot smarter than you."

The end of the road came in sight and Mr. Richards said, "Have you the skills necessary to follow this road to whence we came?"

That struck me funny, those old guys used a lot more of the English language than I did.

"Yes sir, I'm pretty sure there is a distinct chance of success upon arriving at the gate in a timely manner." Piss on the old coot, I'm as smart as that girl any day of the week. He continued looking out the windshield until he dozed off. My message was lost on him. I stopped and opened the gate.

"Back to the ranch young master Winters." Still looking forward he said, "I saw you looking at the saber mounted on the wall. It belonged to my father. He was a Bengal Lancer, he fought the Russians in the Crimean War."

The Russians, the Crimea, Jesus Christ what was he telling me?

"Into the valley of death rode the six hundred, cannons to the left of them, cannons to the right of them volleyed and thundered." It kind of blurted out.

"Very good, only there were 636 men and horses, my guess is that 600 made better prose."

He had my attention now.

"The battle lasted twenty minutes and only seventy men rode back. My father's regiment, the 11th Hussars, better known as Prince Alberts own, was now down to two officers and eight mounted men."

The old man got quiet on the way back to the ranch, quiet like he had a lot more to say, quiet like there was nothing more he could say. All I could think of was wait until I saw my dad, so I could tell him all this. Little did I know, how little I knew?

By the time we got back to the ranch Juaquin had shod the two horses he had said he would, plus two more.

"I would have done those two over there, but I couldn't find any more nails. I just trimmed them."

Just a Mexican, Mr. Richards, was my first thought.

"Why didn't you speak up, Ben and I were recently at the feed store." His voice had raised some, "the mere fact, there was no possible way for you to have a tally on the amount of nails on this ranch is not much of an excuse. I should fire you."

Second thought, what a dick!

Mr. Richards stared at Juaquin for a spilt second, smiled and said, "Juaquin if I still owned this place, I would make you my cow boss and I'd winter somewhere down on the south coast. Thank you, let's go up to the house and maybe have a cool beer. And I will get you some nails!"

Third thought, I didn't know what to think.

The next morning a short time after breakfast, the girl from the feed store drove in the yard and at some volume called out, "Yo rich boy, come unload this truck. I need to go see Maggie." She walked close to me, like she was going to say something, but didn't. She did give me a smile and it was a good one. In the back of her truck were four boxes of various sizes of horse shoes and a keg of horse shoe nails.

Apparently, Mr. Richards was not too keen on the help standing around, due to the lack of parts and pieces.

"Took you long enough." I got the smile again, it was still a good one. As she got in her truck, I was hoping I might get it again, I didn't. All I got was a cloud of dust and some tail lights going down the road.

Mr. Richards walked over to me, "Didn't think to whistle in the cavy this morning and where's your Mexican?"

"No and I don't know." Great way to start a day, getting barked at for doing the right thing and unloading the truck.

"Well, go find him. Your father wants Juaquin to load up that colt he's riding and go to Susanville. He made some sort of deal on a couple of bulls and it may involve that horse, I don't know."

"What about me, what about the grey horse?"

"Nothing, you are not involved."

"What do you mean by not involved."

"Exactly that, you are not involved. Your father said you are to stay and continue looking at the ranch."

Shit, what was I to make of this development? Was something wrong? Was this some sort of penance? I wonder if I should call him and get the skinny straight from the horses' mouth?

"What is the delay, here? Is it possible you could be thinking of ways to get your thumb out of your ass and find that Mexican?"

"Yes sir." He was easy to find. He had whistled Dixie and was standing in among the horses.

Chapter VII

"Benny, that old bird has a yard full of exceptional horses. Look at em, other than some height differences they are all, everyone, built the same. Well balanced, good bone, nice hip and a kind eye. I will be tickled to ride any one of these. You know, did your dad buy them with the ranch?"

"You can ask him yourself. The plan, as I understand it, is for you to load up that colt you're riding and head for Susanville. My Dad made a deal for a couple of bulls."

"Dammit, he has traded that colt. I liked him." We both looked at each other and laughed, that was exactly the move my father would always make. Juaquin loaded the horse and his gunny sack in the truck.

Mr. Richards came to say goodbye and give Juaquin some further instructions from my Dad. Then he was gone and I wasn't. An old man, a rotund Indian woman, and me.

Mr. Richards was saying something to me, I caught the last part. "I need to go to town, find something to do."

Then he too was gone. I kicked a rock in the road. Better find something to do, I guess.

One of the true constants of ranching, is there is never a shortage of things to do. I decided to give some attention to the barn.

That little brain storm used up most of the day and if I do say so myself that ol barn looked pretty good. No one ever accused me of obsessive cleanliness.

Opposite would be a far better way to describe the attitude I held in that regard. However, a belief that things should be organized and in their proper place seemed a good way to view the world.

How long Maggie had been standing there watching, was hard to say, but there she was smiling.

"Snuck right up on you, cowboy."

"Yes ma'am, you did."

"Well, I am an Indian and it's bred into us to put the sneak on you white eyes." That woman had a sense of humor.

"Come on up to the house and clean up for supper. Davey called from town and he is on his way and Davey don't like waiting too long to eat."

"Yes Ma'am."

"You have the ability to put together sentences?"

"Yes ma'am."

"You'd never know it by talkin to you."

"Yes Ma'am."

She smiled, shook her head and walked off.

After dinner Mr. Richards mentioned, "It is time to move the cows to the first pasture we looked at, would you care to be part of the summer migration?" By the way he said it, I knew it was not a question.

Hell yes, I wanted to be part of his summer migration. "Yes sir, thank you for asking."

"Damn it, little white boy, if you don't start talking I'm gonna kick the livin shit out of you, am I clear!"

"Yes ma'am, I shall endeavor to carry on any and all conversations with vigor and reason and take full advantage of all my education in the skills and mannerisms of all good conversationalists." Then showing off a little I added. "Available to me at this stage of my young existence."

"That's a start." Maggie held up her little chubby fist and waved it in my direction.

Who could not like that woman?

Mr. Richards sat in the stuffed chair by the radio, "Ben go get your things and use the empty bedroom upstairs."

That's when I found out there were only two bedrooms in the upstairs and Mr. Richards and Maggie shared one of them. God all mighty, who'd of thought that!

The next morning at breakfast Mr. Richards, after he had put catsup on his scrambled eggs, waved in the general direction and said, "Ben take the truck back up to where we rode and drop off the salt we picked up yesterday and put a new block with the old one. Is that within your scope of expertise? Don't chicken shit it, do it right."

I was thinking more of eggs and catsup than putting out salt. "I can't foresee any problems, Mr. Richards."

Maggie looked up from what I noticed was her version of eggs and catsup.

I wondered who showed who that bit of culinary magic.

"Quit that Mr. Richards shit, his given name is Davey and he has been answering to it for a long time."

"Yes ma'am."

"I believe we have had a discussion on the merits of the spoken word, you little peckerwood."

"Yes ma'am, and in that vein might I inquire as to my chances of getting you to pass me the catsup, so I may be allowed into the world of eggs and catsup, ma'am?"

"When I get done beatin on you a cow pie will be taller!"

At the risk of being redundant, who could not like that woman!

"If the Fibber Magee and Molly show is over, you got shit to do, boy." Apparently, there were different senses of humor at work in this room.

The salt got dropped off in a timely and if I might add efficient, in a non-chicken shit sort of way. I was back to the ranch by lunch time.

Maggie was hard at it in the kitchen, making something that smelled real good.

"Maggie, Jeanie at the feed store said something to the effect that Mr. Richards shot a couple of men somewhere on this ranch. Do you know, or have you heard anything about a story like that?"

"First, I guess maybe you were paying more attention in school than I thought, you seem fairly verbal." She continued, "in reference to the shooting, I don't know much about it at all. It never came up between us. Oh, I've heard all the stories, that's true enough. I guess if Davey wanted to talk it over with me, he would have. He likes you, he might talk about it with you, I can't say for sure. Give some thought to picking the right moment in time to approach a subject as grave as that one no doubt is."

Figure out the exact right moment, how hard is something like that? Harder than Maggie's line about the sailor and the whore house. It didn't look like there be any more information coming from Maggie. She smiled and turned her back. It appeared more important things needed addressing in the kitchen. I guess I ought to go find something else to do.

The next morning Davey said he thought Grey Boy needed a ride and he picked a bay horse he called Jake. "Jake is going to be a dandy. He is coming five and I think he will make a good all-around using kind of horse."

By around one o'clock we had a good little bunch of cows and calves gathered and pointed toward their new home for the summer.

Mr. Richards rode over and asked me if I was capable of taking the cows up this road, we had just crossed?

"Sure, I don't see why not." I said with far more bravado than I felt.

"Normally I wouldn't ask, but Maggie and I are going up to Susanville tonight. I have a dear friend named Sam Hill. He is the local dentist in town and tonight he will be installed as master of our lodge. It won't take you long to get to the gate, the cows know the way. This same road will lead you back to the ranch. Ok."

"Ok."

"Ok."

He put ol Jake into a long trot. It took longer than it should have, of course, but the cows got through the gate to their new summer pasture with no real problems. I waited around awhile to make sure all the cows and calves mothered up. Then I too picked up a trot and headed off down the road. All in all, feeling pretty good about getting the cows taken care of in a workman like manner. If he were around that might get me a pat on the head from Juaquin.

I was enjoying the ride, not paying much attention and maybe even thinking about the girl in the feed store. The road was soft and although we kicked up a lot of dust, we were making good time, when it turned rocky and dropped off steeply. I got Grey Boy stopped easily enough and looked around for another way down. I didn't see one, but what I did see was Jake standing at the bottom. Mr. Richards on the ground with the lead rope from the bosal still tucked in his belt. Jesus, I wonder how long he has been laying there, he didn't look too good.

When I got down to him, his left side wasn't even dirty. His right side, I don't know how to put this, was pointing in all directions and all the directions were wrong! He was laying there so still and motionless and there was a small trickle of blood coming out of his mouth, I thought he was dead.

"That damn horse rolled us down the hill."

I jumped back. "Oh Mr. Richards I thought you were dead!"

"Well, I will admit to having felt better a time or two in my life. Do you think you can help me back on my horse?"

"Yes sir, is it ok if I help you get on my horse? Yours looks somewhat worse for the wear."

"Please tell me I didn't cripple him, that's too good a horse."

"I can't say for sure, he's got a lot of the bark knocked off him and he is favoring his right hind."

"Alright help me on yours, I get the feeling we are in for a long night."

I can't imagine how bad it must have to hurt the old man getting on that horse. He kind of grunted once when I got on behind him and never made another sound for the next two and a half, three hours. Maggie was standing in front of the house when we rode in.

"God damn it, I knew something was wrong." She looked at me, "You have something to do with this?"

"No, he did not!" Mr. Richards held out his good arm. "Help me off this horse and go get the truck, I need to get to town, pretty quick I think."

It was at that moment Maggie informed me she had not the slightest idea of the intricacies of driving a motor vehicle. "It might work better to take him to the truck instead, I can drive."

"We have to go to Susanville, there is no one in town capable of fixing all this." We got him off the horse and into the bed of the truck. Maggie made him as comfortable as she could with some blankets from the house and then climbed in the back with him. I was about to slide into the driver's seat when Mr. Richards held up his arm.

"Ben, unsaddle and grain those two horses. Then we can go, I doubt a couple minutes either way can hurt much. While you are in the barn get that bottle of bust head under the workbench."

Maggie shot him a look. "Whiskey." She said that with some distain in her voice and demeanor. By the time we left it had started to rain a little, not bad. It really started getting after it on the outskirts of Susanville.

Fortunately, the hospital was on the near side of town and we got him in before he got too wet. The waiting room was warm and dry and I dozed off. The next thing I knew Maggie was jabbing me in the ribs. I looked up in time to see this big tall Ichabod Crain looking fellow, in a white coat coming our way. We both jumped up.

He spoke directly to me ignoring Maggie completely. "It looks like your grandpa fancies himself some sort of cowboy, anybody that would let an old man like---." That's as far as he got.

Maggie took a step toward him. "Listen to me you ill-bred, inconsiderate, son of a bitch any and all questions and answers will be directed at me, are we clear!"

God, I loved that woman!

Ichabod took two steps back, "Yes ma'am, we are." He looked at his chart, "Mr. Richards sustained a dislocated shoulder, I popped it back in place and it should not present any problems in the future. He also has two cracked ribs, there again they should heal with no adverse effects. However, his hip is broken in two places and the outlook for a full recovery is grim. I have serious reservations about him walking, let alone riding a horse." He smiled what my mother would have called a smarmy smile, turned on his heel and left.

"You don't know Davey Richards." Yelled Maggie. Then she started to cry.

It turned out Mr. Richards's friend Sam Hill's wife Alma had a sister named Myrtle Williams. Remember Mr. Richards's tale of the guy that burned out the German whiskey seller.

It was the same Williams family and they lived on the next ranch over. I guess that might be the definition of life in a small town. It was quickly arranged for Maggie to stay at the Hill household for the foreseeable future.

Maggie asked me if I minded going back to the ranch and keeping an eye on things until she knew more.

"I'd be happy to do that" I said, but what I meant was shit oh dear. I better call my Dad and get some guidance. This could be out of my league. I got back in the truck and drove back to the ranch.

Chapter VIII

The next morning, I called home, my dad was gone somewhere, and I told my sister as best I could what all was going on. I don't know how much got through to her, but she promised to tell dad when he got home that evening.

The two horses were still locked up from last night and I figured it might be a good idea to check on them in the daylight. Jake was scraped up some but seemed to be walking fine. Maybe Mr. Richards had one less thing to worry about.

A little after eleven in the morning people started showing up and inquiring after Davey and some of them bringing food. Having figured on sustaining life with scrambled eggs and catsup, this turned out to be a boon in my favor. Every one that drove in did not have enough nice things to say about Davey. He was well liked.

Naturally, the girl from the feed store was the one that didn't show. Two things were going on there, a murder story and well, you know some boy girl shit. She had a year or two on me but that shouldn't matter, should it?

The day wore on and people kept coming and going in a steady stream.

A chance to sneak off to the barn presented itself and quick as a bunny there was nothing left of me but a memory. And that's ok, all the people were Davey and Maggie's friends. They didn't know me from Adam.

The thought briefly crossed my mind, one of them surely knew the story of murder and mayhem on the mountain. It was pretty clear this was not the time for any of that and the thought went away.

Late in the afternoon the tide of well-wishers tapered off slowly and then stopped. Maybe the whole town had been represented and there was no one left to come by. Mr. Richards chair looked inviting and at the same time the phone was ringing. More friends of Davey's was my first guess.

It was my dad, "What is going on up there? I heard you ran that old man off the mountain and killed his horse."

"No, no that is not what happened, not at all."

"I know, I'm just pulling your chain." He laughed. "The Indian woman called and gave me the down low. Sounds to me like you did a hell of a job son, I'm proud of you." That wasn't too hard to hear. He continued, "I'm going to need you to stay put a while longer." He paused waiting for me to say something, I guess. "I hired Juaquin's youngest brother Rudy to run the ranch for me, you remember him don't you." I did, sort of. "It will take him some time to get there, he has a wife and two little kids. Tell me your assessment of the ranch and the cows."

That wasn't too hard to hear either. "To me this is a well-run ranch with more effort put into keeping the grass healthy, than over grazing it with a bunch of cows."

"How's the cows look? Sounds to me like they might be thin."

"No sir, Mr. Richards knows how to manage a ranch." I don't know why but I was irritated.

"If what you say is true Benny, Mr. Richards could teach us both a lot." My dad was a born salesman, I wasn't irritated anymore. He went on. "Juaquin told me the horses on the ranch are first rate."

"Yes, they are. Even Jake the one that rolled on Mr. Richards meant no harm. That old man knows horses and brings them along right."

"See if you can get um bought."

"Me you want me to buy them?"

"Why not?"

I was at a total loss for words.

He wasn't. "And buy them right, or I'll kick your ass. I'll call you in a couple of days." And he hung up.

I fell asleep in Mr. Richards's chair and awoke the next morning with a flash in my brain.

There were still cows to be moved and the only clear thought I had, was I have no idea how many there were or even where to look.

For the next four days I was up at dawn and out on the prowl until dark. I got a count on the ones that went through the gate. Mr. Richards would know how many cows he had. I think most of them had been found, I think?

I figured it might not hurt to make one more circle around that side of the ranch in the morning.

The phone rang before I left to get a horse for the morning search. It was Maggie, "Sam and Alma are bringing Davey and me home today, will you please be around to help get Davey in the house? He is still bad off and you know Davey, he refuses to stay another day. Also, please go down to the bunk house and bring up two of the metal beds. Put them on the back porch. You can set that table and the things on it in the back yard. Thank you."

"Yes ma'am, consider it done."

"He got wetter than I thought on the way in and caught pneumonia. That high pocket butt hole of a doctor called it the old man's friend, it will make it easier on him to die." She got silent for a moment. "He ain't going to die! Is that understood?"

It was easy to hear over the phone she was still crying and despite her bravado, still worried. "Yes, ma'am clear as a bell." Quick like, the attack on the bedroom/porch remodel was accomplished in a way that looked workable. It occurred to me that if Mr. Richards saw his horses cleaned up and shiny in the sun he would find some comfort in that. I was hard at it when they drove past the barn.

Mr. Richards head was on his chest and sort of rolling around. He took no notice of his horses.

We got him in the house and set him in his chair, until the women made up the backroom. They were both crying and looked awful.

Sam lowered his voice "Maggie is not doing well with all this right now but have no fear she will. She is one strong woman. I need you to be vigilant and keep a keen eye on the goings on, until she is better. I don't hold out much hope for Davey, pray God I am wrong."

We got him in the back and as comfortable as possible. Sam and Alma stayed a while and tried their best to cheer us up, but mostly they gave each other sad looks. Despite their best intentions, I was glad to see them load up and leave. I think Maggie felt the same. She needed to be taking care of Davey Richards.

"Maggie if Mr. Richards's feels up to it please ask him how many cows were in that pasture? I think I got them all moved, but I don't know."

She jerked her head over at me with fire in her eyes but then softened, "Benny I think you are going to be a good man someday." She looked away, "I'll ask." Maggie had never called me by name before.

I went down to the barn and made some work.

Around dark, Maggie came down and asked me if I was hungry.

"Yes ma'am, I could eat."

She stood there looking lost for a moment, then came over and hugged me, real hard. "I can't, I won't lose that man. God put me on this earth to look after Davey Richards. I can't say why." She hugged me again and shook her head. "Could it be penance for some sins in a previous life?"

"No ma'am, I don't reckon it was punishment brought you here." For the next three days I saddled up and looked for cows and found quite a few.

Maggie rarely left Mr. Richards bed room and when she did, didn't have much to say. On the fourth morning Maggie said Davey was up for some cow talk. "Keep it short!"

"Yes Ma'am, short it will be." She smiled at me, maybe things were beginning to look up. If they were, they weren't looking up much. Mr. Richards looked pale and little. He was so thin it appeared he was floating on the bed and barely hanging on to life. I know I said he looked pale, that might not be the best way to describe it. His face was translucent and took on the appearance of old wrinkled up parchment paper, bathed in sweat and all shiny lookin.

It scared me, I had never seen death and now I was looking at it square in the eye!

"God damn boy, you look pale, you alright?" His voice didn't sound sick. I must have jumped back a little, because he laughed. "I ain't done for, yet."

If that was the case, he had successfully fooled me. Maybe the jury was still out, and the final verdict hadn't been decided.

"Maggie tells me you have been moving the cows to the summer pasture."

"Yes sir."

"What's the count?"

I told him my tally.

"Good job, thank you. If your count's right and I'm sure it is, you are shy twenty head." His voice sounded weaker. "Remember when we rode to the biggest tree in the country?"

"Ya sort of."

"Well, when you find it tomorrow, go directly north about a half a mile until you come to a granite out cropping with some trees around it. There you will find a small trail that leads up hill to a canyon with plenty of grass and water. That's where the cows will be. Got it?"

"Yes sir, I think I do."

"Nothing to think about, just go do it. Now would you please ask Maggie, if she will please bring me a glass of water? I'm wore out. I'll see you later."

I didn't see him for five days. It took two of them to find his 'tree' and another to get the cows out. They were where he said they'd be, and I guess my total was right. I found twenty cows living the good life in that canyon.

Maggie wouldn't let me up in his room for a day and a half. When she did it was very clear, short and quick were key to the deal.

"How you holding up?"

"All things considered, fairly well. How'd the cow search go?"

I guess fairly well was what could be called a relative term. To me he looked rough and if possible smaller and paler than before. Maybe I had a look on my face of disbelief maybe it was something else, I don't know.

Any way he said "Really, I'm convinced the worst of this is in the past and soon enough I'll be figuring out how my sore hip is going to work horseback. Now talk to me about cows and ranching."

We talked for a couple of hours. Maggie checked up on us every once in a while, and seemed content that Mr. Richards was doing ok.

He was amused that I had some problems in finding the 'big tree' but it showed sand that I stuck with it.

A couple of times the opportunity came up for me to talk about buying his horses. I let them pass, truth be told, I plain chickened out. I wondered if the gift my father had of making deals had skipped a generation.

"You cowboys can resume your wild west stories tomorrow." Maggie had put the sneak on me again.

Mr. Richards took a turn for the worse and I didn't see him for a couple of days. When I saw him next, he brought tears to my eyes, I could see there wasn't much left of him. "Come in Ben, speaking of Maggie wild west stories. I have one for you, I suppose you heard about me killing two men on this ranch."

"Yes, sir I have."

"That is not quite right, it was one man." A look of pure pain crossed his face, whether from being sick or the memory of killing a man. I couldn't tell.

Chapter IX

"I buried him not too far from your favorite big tree. You might have rode right over his final resting place." The look of pain left, and he smiled. "But that's close to the end of the story. The beginning of it started in 1862 in what historians call the border conflicts."

That's the God damned civil war he's talking about. I knew little about the Missouri Kansas conflict from school. Kansas was a free state and Missouri had slaves.

"In May of 1862 I was 13 years old. My father raised blooded horses and was successful.

He had 80 acres of good farm land and one hired man named Rufus Waggoner. We had no slaves, my father found it to be an appalling institution. As far as I can see my father only made one real mistake. Of all the places he could have settled after getting off the boat from England he picked Missouri and it cost him, everything.

My father was a God-fearing man and every Sunday we rode four miles to church. He held the Papist in a kind of low esteem and settled on us going to the Methodist church, in his words a good sturdy form of religion.

One Sunday he had a mare in foal and sent me on without him. It was a beautiful bright sunny day. On the way home, I heard some riders coming on the road and pulled off into the trees and hid. It was as I guessed, a small bunch of Kansas Redlegs and they were covering some ground.

My father found them to be morally corrupt and low bred. Although they rode under the American flag and wore the uniform they were not in the army. They were freebooters and thieves.

Typically, onto the farm of a slave holder, a gang of them would ride in. Kill the men and often the boys and sometimes even the women that lived there.

After burning the house and barn, their job turned into stealing anything they could carry, produce, horses, cattle, pigs, wagons, even the poor family's clothes. Mostly of course it was the slaves. Those high-minded sons of bitches stole the slaves not to set them free, but to resell in Kansas.

To a man they would all take off their hat and tell you it was God's work they were doing. Define that as you may.

After they rode by, I got back on the road, I remember thinking how is it that a bunch of thieves and murders can ride around the country side with those stupid red leggings of theirs and nobody does anything about it."

Mr. Richards started to cough and quit talking. "You ok?"

He laid there looking around. I realized Maggie had put the sneak on us, again and was standing there holding a glass of water. How long she had been standing there I had no idea.

After a slug of water, Mr. Richards started again, his voice strong.

"It wasn't all that far to our farm and it never occurred to me to worry after seeing the redlegs. My father was a one hundred percent Union man and had been proud to vote for ol honest Abe.

When I got close, I could tell everything was wrong. I saw the smoke from the house first, then the barn and then my father. Oh God, my father. His body was hanging by one leg from a tree limb and the other leg was bent in an unnatural direction. The closer I got the more bullet holes I could see. Those sons of bitches must have used him for target practice.

I went over to get him down. My father had been a hero of the Crimea, they wrote poetry about him and his kind, he didn't deserve to have a death like this, suffer like this. It was all wrong, there was no reason for a man as fair and honorable as he was, to die so brutally. I didn't have any idea of what I was going to do, but so help me God something was going to get done. I cried for a while before I cut him down. He was hung so low to the ground the blood was caked in his hair.

Somehow, I got him down and while I was trying to clean him up, I saw they had cut off one of his ears. One of his ears, my God. I started crying again."

I looked over at Maggie, she was still as a ghost and slowly rocking back and forth in her chair.

If Mr. Richards noticed, he didn't say anything.

"I guess I was so overcome with it all I didn't realize that one by one from different directions men on horseback had rode into where I had cut down my father".

"What happened here boy?" said one of them.

"Redlegs killed my father."

Another one rode close and got off his horse, he wore a Confederate officer's coat. "That must be the bunch we just tangled with." He put his hand on my shoulder. "If it was them killed your father, we were his avenging angels." His hand felt light as a feather. "We got some of them. Of course, the cowards turned and ran rather than fight. I locked my sights on one riding a fine-looking black horse, but that horse was so fast I missed by a mile."

Nobody really said anything, the men all got off their horses and helped me dig the grave and bury my father. With the exception of a couple that stayed on guard, they all stood by the grave and removed their hats. One of them said a few kind words.

After it was done the officer asked my name. "Davey Richards."

"Richards, Richards forgive me I did not recognize this place, I was here a few years ago and bought a horse from your pa, he was a brit and a good man as I recall." He stuck out his hand and said, "My name is Captain William Quantrill and you are in the company of southern men all devoted to the cause." He got back on his horse and asked, "Well Davey Richards you got a place to go?"

"No sir, I don't" I couldn't stop crying or shaking, I was so cold.

"Get on with that man over there and we'll come up with a plan later." As we rode away it occurred to me my fathers hired man was not there. We rode all night, holed up in a thick stand of trees for the day. Then rode again all night until we got to where I guessed was the final destination. It was just a camp, with a few tents and some cooking fires.

There were twenty or so rough looking men dressed in all manner of clothing. Some had on regular grey army uniforms.

Most of the men did not have on anything even close to resembling a uniform. Instead of uniforms they wore brightly colored shirts with different kinds of embroidery on the front. Small vines of flowers, crescent moons, stars and some had a sentiment stitched in or just a word or two. Most all the shirts had two or four big pockets in the front, made for carrying the extra loaded cylinders for their pistols.

The only things I could see they had in common was most had hair down to their shoulders and they all, every man jack of them, rode big stout well taken care of horses.

As I was sliding off the back of the horse one of the men with our party rode over and said, "Welcome to the world of the bushwhacker, kid. It is not exactly Sir Walter Raleigh, but it works." He got off his horse and opened his coat, he had on a belt with four pistols in holsters and one jammed in the front close to the buckle. He pulled out a pistol the one in front by the buckle. He turned it over in his hand like he was thinking about something, maybe coming to some decision or maybe the circumstances of how it came to be in his possession. Then handed it to me butt first.

"It's a .32 and a good one, it looks well taken care of. If it is of any comfort to you it once belonged to one of the morally corrupted and deceitful red legs that call themselves men, who took part in the killing of your father." It had dried blood on it.

"Oh Davey, Davey," Maggie cried out and made the sign of the cross. She was visibly upset by the talk of a pistol with blood on it. "That's enough for today."

Mr. Richards turned toward us "Yes, it is, maybe tomorrow we can continue." And he closed his eyes.

Maggie and I left the room, she was still bothered and upset. "I had no idea of any of this, no idea at all."

I left her in the kitchen and went down to the barn.

Chapter X

The next day Maggie decided Mr. Richards wasn't up to the task and postponed us a day. I rode up and checked on the cows.

Mr. Richards must have made good use of his day off, when we came in he was sitting up in bed and his voice was strong.

At first no one knew what to do with me, so I just hung around the camp and helped out where I could. Mostly I hauled wood for the cook fires and once in a while helping out whoever was cooking.

One day a man named George Todd, he was a Captain, asked me if I had the ability to read and write.

"You're damned right I can write." I kind of liked and was a little bit proud of the play on words, if he found it funny he made no mention.

"If you are willing I have a good way for you to serve the cause."

"Name it!'

"We need someone to freight goods for us."

"A Teamster?" I wanted to see Redlegs die.

"Well, you would haul freight. The way I see it your real job would be to look around and report back to me about troop movements and strengths. Are the towns fortified, how are the roads, anything you think will help. We figure the Yankee's won't be to inclined to look close at a boy in a wagon, maybe."

"I could do that."

"You still have the pistol Frank James gave you?"

"Frank James, you knew the James brothers?" Maggie interrupted. Mr. Richards got a smile on his face.

"I'd sooner have all the hair on my head pulled out a strand at a time, then disappoint you Maggie. The truth of it is, after he gave me the pistol I only saw him maybe two or three more times. We only spoke a few times and it was brief. Can I continue?"

"Yes please, sorry to interrupt."

"Do you still have it?" it was my turn to interrupt.

"Have what?"

"The pistol."

"No, can I continue now?"

"Yes sir, sorry, please go on."

"I drove that wagon for a couple of months and became a somewhat accomplished spy. Even though George Todd thought it was important I could read and write, that didn't matter. I couldn't write anything down, all my reports had to be from memory. Even though I was young the Federals still held a dim view of secesh spies. If the Yanks caught me at it, my fate was sealed. The nearest tree and a short rope was my future. I would go directly to George Todd and tell him of the things I saw and my opinion of what I had learned. On one of these occasions George took me to a tent towards the back of the camp and in it was this poor bedraggled looking little kid with red hair and freckles. Her hair had been hacked off short and stuck out in several directions".

"Davey, I seem to have this little problem and I think you are the man to solve it. David Richards may I introduce Precious Gem, late of Clay County, Missouri". Captain Todd with great pomp and circumstance took off his hat and bowed low at the waist.

The poor little thing had on ragged bib overalls that were way too big, and what looked like a worn-out long underwear top with several patches on it and no shoes.

Hers was a similar story to mine, except it was Redlegs and the Union Army combined. Some of Quantrill's men found her, close to starvation, sleeping in a ditch. All she had on was a thin flannel night gown. One of the men gave her the bibs and undershirt. She didn't talk much, other than to say Yankees had killed everyone she knew in the world. They knew none of the circumstances as to why she was out there, in the condition she was. After a few days in camp she told George Todd who she was, but not much more".

George continued, "It worked out well with you as my spy, will you give some thought to making her your helper?"

He turned away to leave and as he ducked under the tent flap I heard him say. "Good I'm glad that's settled." She was so pitiful looking.

"Where did you get all those freckles, were you standing behind the screen door when the cow shit?" I thought that would make her smile. It didn't.

"You got some worldly inclination that tells you I haven't heard that said ten thousand times before today."

"What kind of name is Precious Gem anyway?"

"My mother was a romantic." Tears started to fill in her eyes, but that was as far as it went.

"Precious Gem seems a poor name for a rough and tough guerilla fighter." She smiled a little. "It will be an easy name for the Yankees to remember, when they write their history books."

"OK." We shook hands. "I think it might be alright for you and the others to use my last name, it sounds more bushwhacker."

Mr. Richards stopped talking, paused and looked at me. "I don't mean to make light of how quick George Todd put us together. it was a smart move on his part. I was thirteen years old, Gem was twelve almost thirteen. Both of our worlds had been quickly and violently taken from us. Everything we knew, everything we believed in was gone in one afternoon. My father had spoken up for the union and made no secret of his faith and belief in it. Now I wanted to kill every son of a bitch union man I could."

"For about three or four months Gem and I made regular runs throughout Missouri and into Kansas, we even dropped down into Arkansas a couple of times. Captain Todd was right, a couple of down trodden children in a used up old wagon and a brace of equally used up old mules didn't appear to pose much of a threat to the mighty northern solider. Even the low life scum of the home guard pretty much left us alone".

Again Mr. Richards looked over at me. "Benny you must remember even though the country was at war with each other, we were all of us still Americans. It wasn't like we were fighting in Siam or somewhere equally exotic. This is where we lived, everybody spoke the same language, and everybody ate more or less the same kinds of food. Except for the soldiers in uniform people all wore the same styles in dress and attire. Christ all mighty, Benny even though there were many different ways to do it, we all shared the same belief in the same God.

If you got away from the places where the war was going on, it was easy to think nothing had changed and everything was alright. If you had money you could still buy anything. The strings that bound America together came unwound for a while and it is up to young guys like you to never let it happen again".

"One afternoon Quantrill and some of his men rode into our camp to meet with George Todd. They came to start a plan for a big raid and it ended up Gem and I were involved. Quantrill sent one of his men down by the creek, where Gem and I had our wagon and a little camp. The soldier tipped his hat in Gems direction but made it plain he was speaking directly to me. Our presence was required at the officers' tent, immediately if not sooner. We were admitted into the tent with no wait. Captain Todd and Quantrill were talking about a store in Kansas City that would sell pistols to the cause, for Yankee gold, at a highly inflated price.

Gem walked right up to Quantrill and spoke in a bold tone, "Davey and I will go get um for you. Those stupid Federals never check us, we could do you a good job, sir. Quantrill looked at her, George Todd looked at her, then at each other, then at me. They both laughed, and Quantrill said, "is that girl always so quick to let you look into the gates of Hell, Mister Richards?"

What was there to say, that man had heard my name only once and remembered it. I smiled. Quantrill began again. "I had another plan in mind for you two, what do you think George?"

George Todd shook his head slightly. "I don't know Bill, they are awfully young?"

"That is a truism for sure, on that we both can agree." He looked in my direction. "What we want Mister, is for you and this little slip of a girl to go into a certain town in Kansas and tell us, as best you can, about everything on this list." He held out a piece of paper that looked like it had a lot written on it.

"Sir and little missy." He touched the brim of his hat to Gem. "What I need is for you two, to get me all the information you can."

"Sir, I don't want to spy anymore, I want to kill Redlegs not look at them!"

Quantrill's eyes looked sad for the briefest instant and then turned hard and glassy. "I truly understand and respect your motivations, and I suspect you will get your chance soon enough. However, and let me make myself as clear as ice to you. What I need, what the cause needs, is for you to accomplish everything that is being presented to you on this list". He gave the paper to George Todd, left the tent and walked over to his horse. Before he got on the horse, he turned his head back to the open flap on the tent and to all of us inside. Understand?"

I realized I was holding my breath.

"He don't beat around the bush much, does he Davey?" Gem had taken hold of my hand. "We will be proud to do our duty, sir." She turned to George Todd. "Please give Davey the list".

"That's how we found out about the plan to raid Lawrence Kansas".

Mr. Richards laid there a minute like he was gathering up some thoughts. He started in again for a brief moment then quit and started to cough. It was like he could not get air.

Maggie jumped up. "That's enough Davey, that's enough."

"No that's not enough" He looked feverish and was sweating.

"Enough, I said and that's what I meant, God damn it." Maggie was pissed. "There are things to be done and they won't get done with me in here, with you all day."

I wanted to hear about Mr. Richards and Lawrence Kansas, but Maggie was correct he needed some rest. It is hard to find fault in a woman trying to protect her man.

Mr. Richards had fallen asleep.

Chapter XI

That evening my dad called to check in and see how things were going with the ranch and Mr. Richards.

"The ranch is running all right, I guess. Not so good with Mr. Richards, the poor guy is barely hanging on. Dad, did you know that man fought in the civil war."

"No, I had no idea. I mean looking at him it's easy to see he is no spring chicken. You sure?"

"Yes, he is telling his story to me and Maggie."

"How's the horse buying coming along?"

"I haven't got them bought, yet."

My dad didn't say anything. I thought the phone line might have gone dead.

"I did not send you up there to listen to god damned war stories!" This time the phone line was dead, he had hung up. He was right, I knew that. I also knew I would get past my being a chicken shit and make the horse deal. However, it turned out, I mostly knew I had to hear Mr. Richards story.

For the next few days it didn't look like either one would get accomplished. Finally, at breakfast one morning Maggie told me Davey felt up to talking a little and would like some company.

Maggie had spruced him up a little and trimmed his mustache back some. He had lost more weight and his eyes were sunk way back in his head and rheumy looking. He wasn't long for this world, I could plainly see that.

It felt like I was starting to tear up, that wouldn't do, at all. I thought to myself. We both had work that needed to be done.

"Benny good morning."

"Right back at ya." Was he putting on a brave face?

"You and I have a horse deal we need to get done and we will."

"Sure."

" Here we go."

"Gem and I loaded our wagon and started for Lawrence."

"One of Quantrill's men had been a carpenter before the war and had built a false bottom in the wagon and rigged up a spot to hide the pistol near the driver's seat. He did a good job, and no one had come close to finding either one. Most of the time we would load the wagon with some old moldy hay. Sometimes if we could find some, we would load the wagon with kegs of apples or potatoes or anything else that was close to spoiling. The Federal soldiers would stop us and give us a brief look, before sending us on our way. Jim Lanes famous Kansas redlegs would stop us and wave their pistols in our face. Their intention being to show us what scary and awful bad men they were.

Sometimes if they pressed too hard Gem would act like she was about to cry. That made um proud and they would sit up straight in their saddles, smile and laugh. Yes sir, scary bad men, they could make a little girl cry.

When they got done showing us how important they were they would rob the wagon of whatever they could carry.

They always smelled bad and always, I mean always, passed around bottles of cheap bust head whiskey. It took courage to threaten children".

Maggie and I looked at each other and didn't say a word. What could we say, there was nothin to defend.

"The trip to Lawrence was for the most part uneventful. We saw some mounted federals on patrol, we saw no redlegs. At that time on the Kansas Missouri border there were hundreds and hundreds maybe thousands of displaced people walking up and down the roads with nowhere to go. Mostly women and children and their meager belongings. I don't remember if general order number II was in effect yet".

"What was that?" Maggie asked.

"There were four counties on the Kansas Missouri border that the northern government thought had given too much aid to the guerillas. Every single person union or rebel had to abandon their place and move to Kansas City.

"What would you do Ben, if a bunch of soldiers showed up at your folks' place one morning and said move, now?"

A flash of pure anger came over me, I understood.

Maggie squeezed Mr. Richards's hand. "You are preachin to the choir, white man." For the first time in a while, Mr. Richards laughed. Maggie laughed.

"Leave it to Maggie to keep things in perspective. We caused our fate, her people not so much."

"Gem and I camped on the outskirts of Lawrence and drifted in and out. Our thinking was maybe we would not be too noticeable that way. It worked out fine until the day before we were ready to leave and report back with what we had learned about Lawrence and the surrounding area. We got plenty of notice, that day. Our usual method was to take different streets to do our spying. If anyone asked what we were doing, we told them we were lost, and would they show us the way to the mercantile on the main street. We turned up the street and I couldn't believe my eyes".

"Gem that's my father's favorite horse, Lord Nelson, tied in front of that house."

"Oh, Davey how can you tell, there must be millions of black horses?"

"Not with one white sock on his right hind. I want him back, now!"

"Davey should we make a plan?"

"I don't give a tinkers damn about any plan." I jumped off that wagon and ran over to the horse.

"Remember me Lord Nelson?" As I was reaching to untie him I saw my father's sword hanging on the saddle.

"Gem that's my father's sword."

"What the hell you doing around my horse boy?"

I spun around to tell who ever was talking just what in the hell I was doing. It was my father's hired man, Rufus Waggoner standing in front of me. He had on a dark blue uniform with captain's bars on his shoulders. It was fashioned from velvet. His red leggings looked to be made of soft lamb skin. On his head was my father's good dress hat, to which he had thought fit to stick some sort of big floppy feather in the hat band.

This was wrong on so many levels. To steal a man's horse is a hanging offense, to steal a war hero's sword is a moral offense, but to steal and wear the hat of a man that had treated him so well, that's just petty.

"You miserable low life son of a bitch! That is my father's horse standing there!"

"Do I know you boy?" He pulled his pistol and pointed at me.

Out of the corner of my eye I saw the front door open and another man in a high ranking redleg uniform started down the steps toward us with his pistol also pointed directly at me.

When Gem shot at Rufus Waggoner he spun around, either shot or trying to evade being shot and fell down. His pistol went off and he killed the redleg coming out of the door.

Rufus Waggoner had shot his commanding officer dead center between the eyes and he fell hard across Rufus.

I couldn't tell if Gems shot had hit Rufus or not. They were both laying, real still, in a pile at my feet.

People and militia were starting to gather in clumps and coming toward us. Some were trying to figure out what to do. Some were starting to yell back and forth at each other. I saw one soldier pulling his pistol out of his holster and the one next to him was fumbling with his.

It was in that moment of confusion and pandemonium, we had caused, that allowed our escape. I jumped on Lord Nelson and got Gem on the back with me and we rode like holy hell down the road toward the edge of town. A couple of shots whizzed by us.

"Gem, shoot back."

"I can't. I dropped your pistol."

"That may not be too good for our cause; hang on."

The one good of it, that no good bastard had kept Lord Nelson fit and in top shape. We rode that horse hard until we were well away from town and into some woods by a creek, where we could hide.

It was when we stopped, I saw why Gem had dropped the pistol, she had been shot and was still bleeding. This was a bad wound, maybe not as bad as it could have been. How do you explain that, a bullet is a bullet? This one had passed clear through her shoulder but didn't hit bone or any vitals that I could see. It was nothing short of a miracle.

A little skinny girl like that didn't have much in the way of a shoulder. Getting the blood to stop was not all that hard.

Although we made fairly quick work of that, I had no idea how much she had lost. I also had no idea if she was going to live or die. The real problem now was to get back to Missouri.

We had one horse, a good one true, but still only one. We were now, by anyone's definition, real black flag carrying Missouri border ruffians.

Most of the union army and probably every redleg in these parts, would be hot on our trail.

The worst of it though was Gem's shoulder. We had no skills in treating wounds.

Even if there was a doctor here abouts, we could not go to him. We didn't even have a bottle of bust head to pour on it.

Poor little Gem was just a sorry looking ragamuffin with a hurt shoulder and dried blood down her arm and shirt. I felt useless.

"One of the slaves, by where I lived, told me if you burn a scrape it won't get infected."

"Gem how you suppose we go about something like that?"

"Build a fire, heat up the blade of your pocket knife, and lay it on the holes the bullet made, front and back."

"I don't know Gem it's more than a scrape and it can't be all that simple." Really, I was just scared.

"Do it Davey, I would rather have you burn my shoulder than have you watch me die a slow death. Now straighten up and do your job."

I did it. That was the hardest thing I ever done in my life. This was a little girl who instead of wearing frilly dresses and playing with dolls, was laying in the dirt waiting for me to burn her tiny shoulder. I did it, she never made a peep.

The next morning Gem was burning up with fever and saying things that made no sense.

My heart hurt, I knew I had killed her. I didn't want to stay where we were, and I knew we couldn't move. For two days and nights I did my best to keep her comfortable. On the third morning she woke up with a big smile.

"What you got for us to eat, Davey I'm starved."

Laugh was all that I could do, the pure joy of seeing that girl alive. "Well nothin, I can offer you a cool drink of water if you can get to the creek."

Mr. Richards was fading a little and needed to stop talking. Maggie and I could see that, but we both wanted to hear more.

In that instant we went from the civil war and Lawrence Kansas to the present, the phone was ringing in the other room.

Chapter XII

It was Jeanie, the girl from the feed store, there was going to be a dance at the grange hall and was I interested.

"You asking me for a date or just representing the chamber of commerce?"

"I guess that would be up to you to figure out, it'll start at the normal time." The phone went dead.

I thought I was being funny. Why'd she hang up? Was she irritated? Did she still want me to go? Did I even want to go? Is this getting more complicated than it needs to be? I wonder if my Dad---, no.

How many times sittin at the dinner table did Dad say something that cracked me and him up, only to have my mother and sisters just look at us. The thought hit me, he was a grown man and had as much understanding of the opposite sex as I did. Welcome to the world boy.

Maybe I shouldn't even go, but I knew I would.

Have you ever heard the phrase glutton for punishment'?

The phone rang again, oh good we can get this straightened out. It wasn't her, it was the highway patrol.

Some drunk had run off the road and gone through the fence on the main road, about a mile above the house. The highway crew was on the way to fix the fence.

"Thank you, sir that was a thoughtful phone call,".

"I didn't call to be thoughtful, I called because 20 or 30 fucking head of your fucking cows are on my fucking highway and I want them fucking off!" The phone went dead again.

Twice in one day, within a minute of each other, two people had hung up on me. How am I doing so far?

I told Maggie about the highway patrolman's phone call and went down to the barn. As luck would have it there was one horse standing by the feeder and he let me walk right up and capture him. It was Jake, the horse that had rolled on Mr. Richards.

He stood quiet like as I curried and saddled him and stood for me to get on. We started out the gate in the direction of the wayward cows and went smoothly for a couple hundred yards at a trot.

Maybe Jake had some thoughts that ran counter to mine, he did a hundred eighty degree turn and started to gallop back to the barn. He didn't buck, he just ran off. I can't always ride them when they buck, but I can sure as hell ride um as fast as they can run. I pulled him in a fairly big circle and made him run around and around in that circle until he and I got on the same page and started to think alike and lined out.

He tried once more, but not very hard and it didn't take us long to get to the scene of the crime.

About a half a mile up the road from the hole in the fence the highway patrolman and the fence crew had blocked the road with their various vehicles.

The cows were piled up in a big wad against the fence guys' truck. There was a big dent in the door, I hoped it wasn't a new one.

The cows looked as though it wouldn't take much for them to lift their heads and tails and start looking for the proverbial greener grass.

The highway patrolman and the fence crew had made the drunk help them push his car back on the road and were staring at me as I rode up.

The patrolman started to speak, I held up my hand and said. "If you guys can push that car a little farther down the two lane and then kind of spread out and stand quiet, I think I can get them through the hole.

"I'm the officer in charge here, not you kid!"

"Yes sir that's true, but I'm the guy who can get the fucking cows off your fucking highway."

He smiled at that "I hope you are right."

Me too. I eased through the gate and slowly moved towards the cows, once again Jake had different views of the world and he started to buck. I guess the cows were tired and hungry and just wanted to go home.

While Jake and I were jumping around on the black top they walked through the hole in the fence and started to drift away. Jake settled down and I said, "I better haze those cows away from here, see you in the funny papers."

The last thing I heard was the drunk yelling something about the Wild West.

It was dark, and I was hoping Jake had had enough excitement for one day, he had. The ride back to the ranch was uneventful.

The next morning, I poked my head in to Mr. Richards's room to tell him about the cows on the highway.

"Come in Benny, come In." He looked bright and perky, better than he had in days.

That perked me up too.

I related my little adventure of the cows and the highway and Jake. He kind of squirmed around in his bed. I wondered if he was coming back to life.

"I imagine the vocabulary was colorful when Trooper Pederson was describing the scene. He may have tremendous skills in some things, English ain't one of them. Tell me about Jake, how did he do, what do you think of him?"

"Yes sir, I will." I told him the whole thing from letting me catch him, to the run off affair, to the Wild West show he put on for the drunk guy. I finished off by saying even though Jake got a little confused and had some trouble with some of the rules, I thought he was going to be an above average horse.

Mr. Richards lit up I mean he came alive, smiling and wiggling around in his bed. "Benny I couldn't agree with you more, in a couple of days the two of us will start in on him, he will be something." He stopped talking, and laughing, his eyes slowly moved around the room and he said quiet like. "Better go do your chores Ben." He turned and faced the wall.

GEM

I told Maggie about how he had suddenly stopped talking and turned his back on me.

"I guess it is my time of life to cry, Benny."

Later that afternoon Maggie said Davey wanted to tell us some more. He wasn't as chipper, but he started right in.

It had been a couple of days since we had eaten anything, and we were starting to feel some of the affects, but we knew the consequences of capture and didn't dare show our selves. To get back to our camp and safety wasn't all that far by road. However slinkin around in the back country was the prudent and smarter way to go about it. Food or no that was what we had to do. Late in the day we came on a little creek in some thick woods and Gem slid off the horse to get a drink, then froze where she stood. Up the creek on the other side was a big bay horse with a union saddle peacefully grazing and sitting against a tree was a soldier. He didn't move, we didn't move. His horse saw us, threw up his head and started coming toward us.

Gem and I were just glued to the ground, scared shitless. Still the Yankee soldier never moved, his horse crossed the creek and came right up to Gem.

I leaned down and whispered, "That's one sound sleeper. Anyone that sleeps that hard deserves to get his horse stole."

"I don't think he is sleeping." She crossed the creek and walked right up to him. "This federal is talking to Jesus, see if there's anything to eat in his saddle bags."

"Canned peaches, some hard tack on this side and in the off side pocket a bottle of gin wrapped in a uniform shirt. It looks like your soldier was an officer."

"Help me get his pistol and coat and anything else you think we may need. Then we better quit this place, someone is bound to be looking for him."

The soldier did not have a mark on him, if it hadn't been for the open blank look in his eyes a person might think he was asleep. We got his jacket off him and his pistol, he had been a major.

Gem said, "Should we check his pockets?"

"Seems grisly." I found two twenty dollar gold pieces, a pocket knife and a letter.

Gem said, "Leave the letter that's none of our business, take the money and give me the pocket knife."

"Maybe it's a military letter."

"No."

We went deeper into the woods and ate peaches and hard tack. We felt good about robbing the Yankee, then we felt bad about what we had done, then finally agreed it is what it is, and we stopped thinking about it. A day and a half later we were standing in front of Quantrill and George

Todd. Quantrill held up the Lawrence newspaper and showed us the bold headline.

TWO REBEL BOYS ASSASSINATE JIM LANE'S RIGHT HAND MAN

In an act of cold and heartless violence, two young assassins from the lowest form of southern trash executed the second highest ranking officer in the Kansas Militia on Friday and escaped amid a hail of gun fire from the alert and dedicated soldiers of the home guard.

A spirited pursuit commenced and gave chase until the cowardly sons of Beelzebub disappeared into the low swamp
from where they had crawled out.

A reward of $250.00 has been posted for their capture
Dead or alive, preferably dead.

Is there a limit to how far these foul inbred and evil secessionist will sink for their "cause"?

It continued on in the same vein for two full columns on the front page and a couple of related articles on the second page. What it didn't tell us was what, if anything, Gem had done to that counterfeit bastard Rufus Waggoner.

"I see how you got those majors bars on your shoulder, little lady."

"Oh no sir Captain, that's not even close to how it came about."

When Gem and I told those two men the real story of what had transpired on the front porch of that house, up to and including finding the dead yank leaning on the tree. They never said a word until we finished.

Quantrill looked over at the horses and said, "Your father was a good judge of horse flesh."

George Todd got up and walked over to the sword hanging on Lord Nelson. "Your father was a British Officer?"

"Yes sir, the 11th Hussars Prince Alberts Own." I felt about a foot taller just saying that.

"The Crimea, the charge of the light brigade?"

"Yes Sir." Now I felt I was 6 foot 8.

They both looked at each other and then at me and Quantrill said, "I swear on my oath as a southern man and officer in the Confederate Army I will kill that man, Rufus Waggoner, on sight if I ever see him."

George Todd smiled, "I'm not in the army, but I can and will swear the exact same thing.

"Now," Quantrill was back to business. "Tell me what you two assassins learned about Lawrence Kansas."

And we got down to it. Small groups of men started drifting into camp. They were mostly bushwhackers, although there were some regular army troopers and a sprinkling of what I guess were fed up farmers and citizens. There was even a small run down looking hard sided wagon, with a tin roof. Felicity Browns Traveling Revue was painted on the side in faded red letters.

Gem asked George Todd about the wagon and why it was here.

He smiled, patted Gem on the head, "I guess you could say these are women who got lost." And walked quickly away.

I knew what they were, however I lacked the necessary skills, or courage, or even the vocabulary to explain them to Gem. She would find out about all that, soon enough. I took the George Todd way out and said something about checking the horses and left her standing there.

In about a week there were about three hundred or so fighters in the camp. Tension and excitement filled the air. It seemed like you could actually feel it, see it.

Captain Quantrill gathered all the men one morning and gave a rousing speech all about patriots, honor, and free choice. He went on to say in almost biblical terms God wanted us to kill all the Yankees in Lawrence.

Say what you will about William Clark Quantrill that man could fire up a crowd. Every fighting man there was ready and willing to follow him straight into hell and certain death, if that's what he wanted, at a full gallop.

The troops started in on the final preparations for battle. Checking and rechecking the shoes and fitness of the horses. Checking and rechecking and rechecking again their weapons and making sure they had plenty of power and ball. Some of them were holding religious services. Some were passing around bottles of liquid courage. Organized chaos, I suppose it has always been like that, no matter what the war.

Gem and I were getting ready just like the rest, when Captain Quantrill searched us out.

"What are you two doing?"

"Going with you."

"No, no you are not!"

"But sir?"

His eyes lost their hard, focused look, he put his arms over our shoulders and quietly held us. Unlike most of them I could not smell liquor on his breath.

"We are about to embark upon a great battle that will be talked about for years to come. Depending on the outcome of this terrible war it will be viewed as good or evil. What we are going to do in the next few days is more than war, it will be murder plain and simple. Oh, we will try to justify it alright and maybe we will, maybe we won't. However, this turns out it is going to mark the souls of everyone involved and we will live with these actions the rest of our days. I will not do that to you two under any circumstance. Understood!"

Neither one of us made a sound. I told you that man could talk.

"Good, now come with me I need you to do something for me and it involves Felicity Brown."

Felicity Brown was no youngster, the bloom of youth had left her cheeks some years past. She was tall and statuesque and still had a sweet face and the kind of smile that inspired trust. Felicity Brown was also, as I was to find out, a first-class spy and smuggler and gave little thought to the death of any one dressed in union blue.

Quantrill in his formal way introduced us and walked away. I never saw him again, he would be dead and have his head mounted on a pole in about a year. In fact, as I think about most all the rest of the bushwhackers I knew would soon be dead or out of the fight.

"So, you are the two boy assassins that shot up the town of Lawrence and killed that Yankee general."

Gem marched up to the woman, Gems head didn't even come up to her chest. "I am not a boy and I am not entirely sure I shot anybody let alone a general!"

"Well bless your heart, I can clearly see now that you are not a boy." Felicity bent over and picked Gem right off her feet, kissed her on both cheeks and set her down.

"For now, we will leave the story as it is, the south could use a hero or two".

The three women traveling with Felicity gathered around Gem laughing and giggling and generally acting, well, like girls. My first thought was, I hoped their intent was not to teach her the tricks of their trade.

"She'll be fine, they are going to clean her up and fuss over her some. I doubt you've done much of that." She was right. "Come over here and join me inside the wagon it's cooler in there and I'll fill you in on what we are going to try to accomplish for the war effort."

The inside of the wagon looked nothing like the outside.

It could have been a room in a fine house complete with dark wood paneling and brass lamps. Across the front was a bed built on a platform that had pull out drawers, with brass handles. On one side was a table that fastened to the wall when not in use. On the other was a bench inlayed with little tiles that formed a picture of a blue bird in flight. At the end of the bench mounted on a very ornately carved wooden stand was a small wood burning stove.

What I thought was how do four women travel, let alone apply their trade in these cramped quarters. What I said was, "ma'am, this is really something in here."

"Yes, it is. I will admit at times it gets a bit cramped. As you can well imagine."

"I can. I traded a pretty little octoroon girl, I picked up in Shreveport, to an Armenian Jew for it back after the war started." She waved her arm around giving me the grand tour. "How did I do?"

"OK I guess." I had to think about that one. I knew slavery was legal, hell that's what all this war and death was all about. The picture in my mind was of a pretty young girl and a fat old man with bad intentions. I, of course, have no idea if that was the case. It could well have been a homely girl and a handsome young man who wanted to tell her stories from the bible.

I was never completely sure on how I felt about slavery, until that day.

Sometime during the night, the fighters left in one direction and in the morning, we went in the opposite direction. The dainty birds, as Felicity referred to them, had done the best they could on Gem. In their line of work, they didn't have a lot of things for little girls. They had managed to find her a clean shirt and combed out that wild red hair of hers, as best they could.

Felicity rummaged around in the wagon and came up with a new looking bowler hat that fit pretty good. I can't say why, but Gem took to wearing hats the rest of her life, although that particular one didn't last all that long.

Gem refused to give up her officer's coat even though it was way too big and cumbersome. Felicity allowed that maybe it was a good idea to keep the coat, where we were going our chances of running into federals were pretty good.

Our mission as it turned out was pretty much what Gem and I had been doing all along, excepting the combination of Felicity and the dainty birds added the ability and opportunity to gather a lot more information than the two of us could and in a whole different way.

Mr. Richards interrupted his narrative to look at me and Maggie. "I guess you know what I mean?" He was talking to Maggie not me. "I have a little more in me if you want?"

Again, he was talking more to Maggie than me.

"Let's knock it off for the rest of the day, what do you say?" He nodded and we left his room.

Chapter XIII

I admit the part about the dainty birds had captured my imagination. I didn't think it was a subject Maggie would have much interest in.

"Can you imagine being about your age and living with a wagon load of women, let alone women that had fallen so far from grace?" I guess she was interested and yes, I was trying to imagine a deal like that. I must have smiled or something because she smacked me on the back of the head. "I am sure you have some chores to do, get to it!"

I decided the dance might be some fun and I didn't think that a little dancing and snuggling up with Jeanie could be all that bad.

When I told Maggie my plan she laughed and said. "Oh, that will be so much fun I would love to go."

That wasn't how I had it figured.

"But I can't, I need to stay with Davey. You go, maybe Jeanie will let you brush up against her while you two are dancing. I suspect that's something you'd enjoy."

Yes, I would. "You sure you won't go?"

"I am pretty sure you will be able to soldier on without me."

"Yes ma'am, I'll give it my all." I got all slicked up, put on a clean shirt and brushed the dust off my hat. I wanted to make a good impression, so I decided I couldn't do better than show up on a flashy shined up colt. I picked Jake.

I spent considerably more time brushing and working on making the colt look good than I did on myself. When I was satisfied how first-rate he looked. I saddled up and rode down the lane to the highway. At the intersection of our road and the two lane I stopped for a Model A pickup loaded with Mexicans, I assumed were also headed for town and the dance.

I was not paying much attention to the pickup or its load, mostly I was thinkin about the good impression I was going to make with Jeanie when I rode up on this good looking well made horse.

As they went by the Mexicans held up their beer cans and waved at me and Jake.

I smiled and waved back. All the waving and beer drinking didn't seem to bother him much, but when the truck backfired his whole view of the world changed. This was not what he had signed up for. He reared up and spun around so quick, I literally flew out of the saddle and slammed onto the ground.

My first thought, of course, was I hoped those guys in the Model A hadn't seen me bite the dust. The second was my horse, who was in the process of showing me what a good job I had done on brushing out his tail.

By the time I got up off the ground he was out of sight and headed back to the ranch, I hoped.

My shirt was ripped and my shoulder besides hurting like hell didn't feel right. There was nothing to do but start walking.

One of my dad's favorite sayings was, if man was meant to walk, he'd of been born with hooves. Right now, I found no humor in it.

By the time I got to the ranch, I once again had two thoughts. One I hoped Jake was alright and standing by the hitch rack and two what had I done to my shoulder, it was on fire.

Maggie came out of the barn holding a halter and noticed me standing there.

"What's wrong cowboy?"

I just looked at her.

"Got your shoulder when you bucked off?"

"Yes, ma'am guess I did."

She came over to me and said, "Lay down right where you are."

I did, and she grabbed my arm and stuck her foot in my armpit. "This will hurt."

Ever heard the saying, truer words were never spoken?

After Maggie jerked on my arm and put it back in the socket where it belonged, it still hurt but not as much.

"You'll live, let's go take care of your horse cowboy."

All thoughts of showing off the horse to the girl dimmed.

"Benny don't get it in your head those women passed me around like I was some sort of potentate with his harem, that's not the case at all. That's how they earned their living and Felicity made it clear no free rides were allowed or tolerated."

He had started right in with no preamble at all, which led me to believe Maggie and Mr. Richards may have had some sort of heart to heart about how much information a teenage boy needs to know on the occupation of tainted women.

"However, I will say these women had long ago given up on modesty and most of my education on the female anatomy came from my time with them."

"That might be enough on the subject of loose women and young boys." Maggie wasn't liking where the narrative seemed to be heading. "He has plenty of time to learn of such things."

That could be true, I guess, but as they say there is no time like the present.

Mr. Richards looked at me and smiled he wasn't so old he couldn't remember what goes on in a boy's head.

We were headed in a south westerly direction, Felicity never actually told us the final destination or who we were to give our information to. Sometimes Gem and I would ride on ahead and look around. Sometimes I would go alone. Always, always when she and the birds had, as she called, its espionage or intrigues to do with any soldiers or teamsters or any stray anybody that we came upon with money to spend, she would tell us to go on a scout.

GEM

She gave me a pair of binoculars she had taken in for a turn on one of her girls. Inscribed on a brass plate on the side was Colonel I. S. Quick, 6th Vermont Infantry The dainty birds smiled among themselves when she gave them to me.

I thought they were smiling because Felicity was being nice to me, that wasn't it.

The days ran on together, day after day. The weather was pleasant and balmy. Sometimes we avoided the war, though not always.

It was all around us, a couple of times we came on groups of tired and sad faced Negro men digging graves and putting the dead from both sides in the same holes. On one stretch of road there were dead men, horses and carnage all around us and nowhere was there a single living thing anywhere in sight. There weren't even any birds. Just the most terrible overwhelming smell. It attacked our senses and permeated our clothing and hair, it worked its way into our bodies and mind and stayed. To this day I cannot forget it. It was a rare day we didn't hear gun fire coming from somewhere.

I could see Felicity and Gem were growing close and becoming friends. Hell, I liked her too. I had no illusions of what she was, who she was, that was common knowledge.

Who knows what set of circumstances drove her to this life, maybe she wanted to live like this maybe it was something else.

It didn't matter to me at all, as far as I could tell she was a good woman and the fact that she and Gem were becoming pals was alright with me. Poor little Gem had lost everything in her world and if an aging prostitute and sometimes spy brought her some happiness and comfort, I could not find fault in that.

I decided to keep the trading the wagon for the girl story to myself. We strung together three peaceful days in a row and I rode ahead. About a mile from the wagon the road went up the side of a hill. With the Colonels glass I could look back and see Gem sitting on the wagon seat next to Felicity. They were laughing and carrying on apparently without a care in the world.

The wagon was coming slowly forward up the road toward me and then it stopped.

Three men rode out of the trees, one of them rode up to Felicity's side of the wagon and started talking. I didn't think much of it, that's what Felicity did. I could plainly see they were southern men and guerillas. The one doing the talking had a scalp tied on his bridle and what looked to be another one fastened to his boot top.

Like I say I wasn't paying much attention, then I was. The man pulled his pistol and shot Felicity in the chest. I saw a little puff of smoke come off her dress. She rolled from the wagon seat real slow and landed on her head, then crumpled on the ground against the wheel. I think she was gone before she hit the ground. She laid there so still, with the breeze blowing her dress around.

True violence is always quick, but it wasn't over. Just as quick the three men were shot off their horses and were laying on the road next to Felicity. A dozen or more Federal troopers rode in from the other side of the road.

Maybe one minute had passed maybe it was two and four people were dead. Gem was nowhere in sight. I had to get down there!

I came galloping down that road as fast as that horse could run and slammed to a stop before I realized every soldier there had drawn his weapon and were waiting for the order to open fire. I didn't care I had to find Gem.

Gem was yelling "Don't shoot, don't shoot, please don't shoot him!" The officer in charge looked at me then at the dainty birds and finally at Felicity on the ground. "Who is he, who are they, and who was she and what about that pistol the boy has?"

By the time the rest of the Yankee detachment arrived, the officer had more or less figured it out in regard to me and Gem.

After talking it over with his two junior officers he came back and told us. We could keep the wagon and mules and ordered his sergeant to give us a couple of boxes of army rations. He asked us if we would trade the three dead rebel's horses for the one tied on the back of the wagon with the US brand. Even though he shouldn't, he said I could keep the pistol and my father's sword. His men buried the rebels and Felicity by the side of the road.

Gem being more inclined toward religion than I, asked the officer if she could say a prayer over Felicity.

As I stood over her with my head bowed, I thought about Felicity spending all of eternity lying next to her murderer. That did not seem right, at all.

The officer and his men loaded up the dainty birds and their things in one of his wagons. He smiled big and told us there is a war on and people with specialized trades like these three lovely ladies had, are hard to find and in high demand. The officer nodded to Gem, lined his men out and rode away with military precision.

In the overall world of war and its destruction these events of today were not much more than a short after-action report describing the actions of his men, the rebels and an old whore. For the longest time Gem and I sat in silence, by the road, looking at the graves.

"Davey why did that federal turn us loose?"

"What do you mean?"

"Davey that man is our sworn enemy and we are his, yet he treated us with kindness. That horse with the US brand, you carrying the dead yanks pistol, we were in the company of rebels and rebel women with known sympathy's to the southern cause. He was within his rights to shoot us where we stood, and he didn't. He left us with everything we had. He even took that worn out horse we got from the dead Yankee and left us three good ones. He didn't even ask where the horse came from"

I didn't know how to answer her. I just saw a man who I believed loyal to our way of thinking shoot a woman who was truly loyal to our ideals and beliefs. I also witnessed a man whose thinking was utterly and absolutely opposed to me and Gems whole world treat us with respect and dignity.

After a while we climbed up on the wagon and started down the road to where we had no idea. We didn't find the money in the wagon until later. I can't say Gem and I made any conscious decision to quit the war, just the farther away from it we got the better we felt. We hadn't seen a soldier or dead body or heard any of the sounds of action in four days. It was so peaceful and quiet.

For the first time since we met, Gem and I relaxed and enjoyed where we were, who we were. Gem the little guerrilla fighter was showing me a side of her that sparkled and shined in the light. Precious Gem, if her mother could only know.

The war came back, blocking the road were two heavily armed men. I stopped, and they rode closer, I could see one of them was a kid not much older than me. He was the one that demanded in a high voice, "Where'd you get the horses tied on the back of the wagon?" I have been in this war long enough to know how I answered could mean the death knell for me and maybe Gem. I just sat there.

Three more men rode up from the back of the wagon and looked at us, waiting for my answer I guess. The older of the two in front asked a little softer, "Where is Felicity, is this not her wagon?"

Gem didn't wait or think how to answer, "Yes this is her wagon and those horses belonged to the filthy low life vermin that shot her down in cold blood!"

"I suppose it was you two dispatched the owners of the horses?" The kid in front asked.

"No it was Yankees."

"You expect us to believe that."

"Believe what you will." Gem was on fire and if the sparks coming from her eyes were lethal that boy would be in big trouble.

"Wait", the older of the two held up his hand, "Shit, Jesse I know these two." He rode up close to me and took his hat off, "I helped you bury your father." He put his hat back on. "These two are the famous assassins that shot up Lawrence before we got there. If we had more like them, we would not be losing the war. By the way I heard it was a hell of a shot that brought down that Yankee bastard."

I should have spoke up to tell them what really happened, but I didn't. Not a lot of the night we buried my father is clear in my mind even to this day, but I do remember who gave me the pistol with the blood on it and I was lookin at him.

"Quantrill told us of the oath he and George Clyde made to you. I want you to know every man jack of us rode into Lawrence looking for that man. I cannot tell you we succeeded, although it was not for lack of effort. We got a lot of them that day."

His eyes lost focus and he looked down at the ground, when he looked back at me I thought maybe I saw tears in his eyes. That brought back the memory of the last time Quantrill and I spoke and I knew at that moment, he was right. He had given me a great gift.

"Where you two headed?"

"I don't know, I don't even know where we are right now."

"Well, you are in Arkansas and I know if you keep on in this direction you will eventually get to Fort Smith. From there, if you turn right, the road leads clear to the Pacific Ocean. By the way the federals have upped the bounty on you two, to five hundred Yankee dollars."

"Five hundred dollars?"

"That's each."

"One thousand dollars for us?" Gem and I looked at each other in disbelief.

"Yup, that fellow you shot up was a very important member of the military and a rich, powerful politician in the Kansas legislation. He might have even been next in line to be elected to go to Washington."

One of the men that had stayed in the back rode up and handed me a small flyer. "Here you go kid, a souvenir from Lawrence."

It was a wanted poster of me and Gem. The likeness drawn on it showed two young desperadoes that looked so mean and despicable, I could easily picture them not only killing someone but probably eating their livers, as well.

The man that handed me the poster pointed at the James brothers and said. "I believe you two are more famous than they are."

With that each one of them rode up and shook my hand, tipped their hat to Gem and rode away.

"Notice they never got off their horses and never stopped looking around."

"I did, a bushwhacker, it seems, is a job with no time off and little opportunity for advancement." "Is that our future?"

Of the two of us Gem was always the smarter. "You ever seen the Pacific Ocean, Davey?" "Maybe an idea like that warrants some thinking on our part?"

It occurred to both of us, pretty much at the same time, the Pacific Ocean was just too farfetched to really think about. I picked up the reins and we started down the road.

"I look much more ferocious than you in this picture."

"How do you know that one is you and not me?"

"Is it harder to picture the Pacific Ocean or the thought of the two of us being famous pistol fighters?"

Gem tore up the poster and let the breeze take the pieces. We moved south and managed to avoid the war for a couple of days.

On the third day it caught up with us again, in the form of a troop of federals. The captain in charge was very polite when he asked us to keep our hands in plain sight and to explain our reasons for being on this road at this time. Before we could answer he asked us if we would mind getting down from the wagon and allowing his men to search our wagon.

We climbed down, and I figured we were going to get shot, politely. The cavalryman that was searching the inside of the wagon came out very excited and said, "I knew they were secesh trash." He was holding my father's sword and our pistol.

"Thank you private."

Gem and I were surely doomed now, but what caught and held my attention was how black the private's teeth were.

"Private will you please give me the pistol and put the sword back in their wagon."

"But sir."

"I have every confidence we have enough men and experience to fend off a saber attack from either one of these two, would you agree private."

"Yes sir."

To us he said, "Will you please remount your wagon and fall in with the troop?" To Gem he asked, "Are you Felicity Brown?"

At least the fellow with the black teeth didn't get to shoot us, yet. It didn't take long to get to the small town the Yankees were occupying. The captain directed us to tie up our wagon and spare horses in front of the livery and follow him to headquarters. Once inside he pointed to a bench against the opposite wall and told us to wait while he reported to the commanding officer.

Gem poked me, but I had already seen it. Exactly above our heads, where we were to sit down, mixed in with the various notices and proclamations was the wanted poster of the two of us. This one said we were worth more money than the last one we had seen.

Maggie and I were listening to Mr. Richards's story so intently neither one of us heard the knocking on the front door at first. It was my father wanting to see some of his new ranch and my mother had come along for the ride.

Chapter XIV

After all the introductions were made, Maggie asked who was hungry and went off to the kitchen with my mother.

Mr. Richards said it was time he took a little nap.

My dad said, "Show me around and show me these horses I've been hearing about."

"Sure."

"Got em bought yet?"

"Not yet."

I knew once we got to the barn and I whistled Dixie, he would become a little more insistent. When the horses came in, right on cue, I was right; he did.

"Have you put a ride on all of them yet?"

"Yes, I have, and there ain't a bad one in the bunch."

"Show me the one got your shoulder."

How'd he know about that? I pointed out Jake. "Despite the fact he and I had a brief parting of the way, I believe he is the best horse on the place; I really like him."

"How come you have not made the deal to buy them and don't give me a line of bullshit about listening to his war stories."

"Dad that's not how it is, well, that is how it is but that old man is not just telling war stories. I have no intention of running up against you and still intend to get the horses bought. I have all my life to buy horses, I do not have all my life to listen to what that man has to tell. God damnit Dad I will never be in on that kind of history again."

My father just looked at me for a minute or two. Kind of smiled, "Tell me about the rest of the horses."

Although we would never talk about it the father son dynamic changed a little that day. We talked horses all afternoon and had a great time. Before he and mom got in the car to leave, he told me to handle the horse deal as I saw fit and shook my hand.

The next morning Jeanie from the feed store drove in the yard with a set of crutches in the back of the truck.

"I heard you got yourself hurt on the day of the dance."

"A little, I guess."

"Why didn't you call and tell me what was going on, that you were hurt?"

That caused me to bristle up and think about pushing back, but before I could she put her hand on my cheek.

"Ben I'm not telling you what to do, I'm telling you I care what happens to you." Now my brain went another direction. "You seem all heeled up now, get those crutches out of the truck and take them inside."

That put me back to thinking about a whole different set of things. Jeanie put her hand gentle like on my sore shoulder, looked me square in the eyes, and smiled.

This set off a whole different kind of brain wave. Maybe life would be easier as some kind of monk in the Gobi Desert?

I got the crutches and Jeanie left down the road in a cloud of dust, again.

Maggie asked me to help Mr. Richards get out of his bed and sit in the sun for a while.

"Sunshine can cure anything that ails you."

With the help of the crutches, Maggie and I got him outside and sitting with his face to the sun. He looked so pale and little I had doubts he would have the strength to get back in bed. I was wrong.

"Benny go start the pickup and take me down to the barn."

"I better go talk to Maggie."

"You better talk to me God damn it, I never had a mother and it is a little late in the game to start now!"

I will say that brought a little color to his face and I guess he might have looked some better. I got the truck, loaded him in and we drove down to the barn.

"Thank you." He pointed to the corrals. "Now go whistle Dixie, I want to look at some horses."

Maggie was not too pleased by my actions with Mr. Richards, but I think she understood.

Later that afternoon he crutched into the kitchen and visited with Maggie and me and asked if it would be alright to continue his tale, as he put it, sitting in the back yard in the morning.

We only sat there a minute or two before the door to the office of the Major in charge opened and we were summoned. He was starting to run to fat and looked tired and worn, but he was clean shaven and his uniform freshly pressed.

"Where did someone like you come by a sword like this?"

"Someone like me? That saber was carried proudly by my father, in the Crimea!"

"You going to sit there and tell me your father was a Bengal Lancer?"

"Prince Alberts own."

"And where might this hero of English gentry be now?"

"Moldering in his grave for close to a year."

"Oh, and how did this awful event occur?"

I wanted to ring this Yankee bastard's fat neck. "Being in the wrong place at the wrong time. He was an outspoken Union man."

"You saying rebels killed him?"

I didn't answer, I looked down at my feet instead. He didn't speak for a minute then looked at Gem.

"Why do you have this weapon, boy?" He pointed at the pistol.

"I am not a boy!"

"Oh, begging your pardon ma'am, I meant you no offense, just answer the question."

"It's the times we live in, sir."

"Explain that little lady."

"It is quite simple you can get in trouble for having one and you can get in trouble for not having one, just as quick."

The Major had to think that one over. "The case for that could be made, maybe." He looked back at me. "I can only assume neither one of you is Felicity Brown. Please explain how it is you two came to be detained while driving her wagon?"

Gem spoke right up. "Felicity Brown was my grandmother and she was a songstress of some repute."

"And Miss Brown the songstress is not in your company because?"

"She too has shuffled off this mortal coil."

"Oh."

"Yes sir, rebel trash shot her off the wagon seat, right next to me." Gem clouded up and started to cry a little.

The major quickly looked at me. "May I ask where this happy little family was headed?"

"The Pacific Ocean."

"The Pacific Ocean?"

"Well eventually, right now we were bound for west Texas. It was important to her to get us out of this war and we understood the war had not reached west Texas yet."

"It has, and it sounds as though she has succeeded in escaping the war." He reached in a drawer and pulled out a cigar and a form that he signed, then leaned back in his chair and lit the cigar. "I don't know if this is one of the sad tales of children and war or if it is total cow flop. I don't care. Take this pass, go get that wagon and leave this part of the world. I truly hope you find the Pacific Ocean, I suspect it is more pleasurable than west Texas."

"Gem what made you think of the grandmother part?" She didn't answer, she pointed at the wagon. Someone had untied the horses and they were tied in the corral next to the livery.

"If you will take the saber and pistol to the wagon, I'll go get the horses." I opened the gate and started to untie the horses when I heard a voice behind me.

"What do you think you are doing with my horses, sonny?"

I turned around to see where the voice came from.

Leaning on the fence, down a ways from the gate I had come in was a scrawny man with a huge pipe in his mouth that was producing a good deal of smoke and a filthy misshapen hat.

"Your horses?"

"That's right sonny, mine! I would, however, entertain any offers of a quick sale or trade."

"You want me to buy my own horses from you?"

"You catch on quick, sonny. I will take a trade or money, it is up to you."

"I would be more than happy to trade those horses for a round piece of lead." Gems voice was soft, when she cocked the hammer it was loud.

I had not seen her walk up or jam the pistol in the livery man's back and it was pretty apparent neither had he. The pipe fell out of his mouth, still smoking, into the mud and horse droppings he was standing in. He just stood there, still as a statue, looking scared. I guessed we were pretty close to working out an agreement on his trade. I gathered up the horses and came to the gate.

"Sir, it seems a shame that fine pipe of yours fell in the mud, maybe you should give some thought to getting down there in the mud and looking for it?"

He dropped to his hands and knees.

"Sir, might the search go easier, if you got a little closer to the mud?" He stretched out to his full length in the mud.

I tied the horses to the wagon. Gem got on, I started to, but instead I ran back over to the livery man and jammed his face in the mud with my foot.

"That's a side of you I've never seen. I like it."

"You're the one, the famous pistol fighter, whose picture is on the wall."

We pulled out and started down the road. We plodded on moving in a southwesterly direction. The weather held, and we had no contact with the war or fighters from either side for about three or four days. We kept to more or less the same routine that Felicity Brown had set up. One day I would ride ahead, the next Gem would.

Even though it would be a stretch to think of ourselves as still spying for the cause, faithfully we still took I.S. Quick's spyglass with us on each ride and scoped out the surrounding country side.

Ever the vigilant one Gem spotted the burned out house first. It was about a mile off the road hidden, somewhat, in a stand of pecan trees.

"That might be a good place to spend a couple of days and rest up the livestock, what do you think?"

What was left of the house sat on the top of a small hill and was just as it looked from the road. Down the backside of the hill was the barn with most of the roof intact. A good sized fenced in pasture with a creek running through it and a small garden.

"Look alive, Gem this place may be occupied."

I pulled the wagon into the barn, checked the fence and turned out the horses and mules into the pasture.

"I better look around some."

I didn't look long, on the back side of the barn was the occupant, I guess. He was leaning against the wall and as I turned around, I saw about ten feet away two more dead bodies. This sounds awful, I know, but all that occurred to me was how many graves am I going to have to dig in my life? I heard a noise behind me and spun around raising the pistol. It was the man leaning against the barn, he was still alive.

"Gem I'm going to need a hand." We got him in the barn, but we could not lift him in the wagon. We took a blanket from the wagon and laid him on it, on the ground. That's all we could do for the poor man. I went around back and started digging.

Gem got a fire going in the stove, in the wagon to boil some water. Through the wall of the barn, I could hear the wounded man moan from time to time.

The two fellows I was about to bury didn't look all that much older than me. By the time I finished Gem had cleaned up the man as best she could.

"He has lost a lot of blood and I think he was shot twice. Once in the upper part of the leg, there is a hole on the other side, so I guess that one went clear through. I would also hazard a guess based on our past, it is something we are more than able to attend to." She lifted the blanket and pointed down low on his side just above his hip bone. "I'm not as confidant on this one, the bullet is still in there." "You think we could burn it like we did your shoulder?" That seemed a long time ago and a lot of miles.

"I think we got to get the bullet out first. Then burn him."

"Gem."

"I felt it, it's not that far in there. We probably best not wait, we should get right too it."

"We?"

"I'll do it." And she did. I held him down while Gem stuck her finger in the hole and fished it out. The man never made a sound, once he opened his eyes and looked at me. He did cry out when we laid the hot knife against his skin, in three different places. I don't think anyone would think less of him for that.

"Davey you think he will survive?"

"He looks peaceful now."

"I think I'll clean up in the wagon and take a nap, this act of being a doctor kind of took some of the starch out of me. Keep an eye on him." She climbed up in the wagon and shut the door.

I sat down next to the wounded man and felt his forehead, it was hot.

GEM

Gem opened up the door and stuck her head out. "Davey, I think you better come in here." She was sitting on the bench by the stove. "Come all the way in and close the door."

"What's on your mind?" She knelt down in front of the stove, down by the fancy carved base and pushed on one of the flowers engraved on it. It was a door and it popped open. Inside was a bottle of brandy, two small pistols, an envelope and a canvas satchel. Gem reached in and handed me the envelope, set the pistols and the brandy on the floor and slid out the satchel.

"Open it, Gem."

It was full of money, mostly Yankee green backs, but some Confederate and even some foreign money. Felicity Brown was a frugal woman.

"What's in the envelope?"

To whom it may concern,
This letter is to introduce Mrs. Felicity Brown a patriot and true daughter of the south. Please extend any and all courtesies available. She does the good work that is needed for us to prevail in our struggle.
General Robert E. Lee
Commander, Army of Northern Virginia

We didn't say anything for the longest time. "I guess she wasn't just some old worn out prostitute after all."

"No, I don't believe that's the case."
"What do we do with this?" she pointed at the satchel.

"Nothing now, put it back where you found it. We don't need any of it, at this time."

"Davey there is no way we can explain this money, if someone asks us, no way."

Gem and I at that instant became rich and poor at the same time. Of all the problems and woe that could beset a person, I'll bet no one would ever hold up their hand and say a bag full of money might be the worst thing to ever happen to me.

She started to replace 'our' new found plunder. "Davey there is another little door back here." This compartment opened under the bench next to the stove. In it were two brand new, never fired Henry repeating rifles wrapped in oil cloth.

"Take your nap, I'm going to look at your wounded man."

His eyes were open, watching me come out of the wagon. I wondered if he had heard me and Gem talking about the money. Jesus, is that what money and guns do? I didn't know about it five minutes ago. Now I was worried someone was going to take it.

"Who are you?" His voice was weak, but his intent was clear. I believed him to be a man of authority.

"Please sir, I mean you no disrespect, however it was you, I found wounded with two men lying dead at your feet. Mister, they were more boys than men. There is some chance the only reason you are breathing Gods pure air is a direct result of our actions. Given that, I suppose it would be considered polite for you to commence with the introductions and fill us in on the story line."

He looked up at me. "Our?"

"Talk."

"If my coat is still around, look in the breast pocket and tell me what you find." It was a badge engraved with the words 'Special Deputy'. "I have been voted on and hired by the city of Lawrence Kansas to hunt down as many of the perpetrators involved in that infamous raid, that I possibly can."

My heart sped up.

"My primary task, the one I am most committed to, is finding and bringing to trial the two boys that so wantonly and in cold blood, committed murder on our leading citizen."

My heart may have stopped. "Is that the two I just buried?"

"I am reasonably sure it was them. It doesn't matter much if it was them or not, a dead rebel is a dead rebel. You seemed to have been in a big hurry to plant a couple of them in the green earth.

"I don't know that I was in any particular hurry, it needed to get done regardless of their war time beliefs."

"How am I to get my reward money?"

"Dig them up, if you want."

"What led you to believe in those two?"

"One of them was mounted on a black, with one white sock."

"You killed two boys because one of them was riding a black horse?"

"A man named Rufus Waggoner was there in the hail of gunfire produced by the two cowards and saw the whole thing. He gave me the description of the horse."

"Just out of idle curiosity, if that man was so close how did it happen, he was not murdered at the same time?"

"It was one of those war time miracles, I guess, not a scratch."

"Not a scratch, you say?"

"A good thing too, as it turned out he knew one of them from his time in Missouri and could name him. David Richards."

Mr. Richards looked over at me.

Chapter XV

"Benny help me back in the house, I am all tired out." He left me hanging over the preverbal cliff on purpose, I took that to be a sign he was starting to feel better. I tried to think of some kind of reason to go in to town and see Jeanie at the feed store, I couldn't. Maybe I should call her, I didn't. I went down to the barn and caught a sorrel mare Mr. Richards called Lucy and rode out to look at cows. Wondering why I was so chicken shit about that girl. The next morning Mr. Richards got out of bed, dressed, and with the help of his crutches made it out to the back of the house before we knew he'd done it.

When I discovered him, he was sitting on the tree stump that was used to split fire wood.

He was chewing on a cigar and when he pulled it out the end was wet and soggy. "I used to go through a lot of these like this, I was never tough enough to smoke them."

To my way of thinking it would have been easier to light one up, than eat the damn thing.

"I want $40.00 per horse."

"Sir?"

"Losin' your hearing boy?"

I had heard my dad say, maybe you need to sharpen your pencil, on more than a few occasions. That's what I said to Mr. Richards.

"Sharpen your own God damned pencil, you want to buy some horses or not!"

"Yes sir, I do."

"Then stop trying to talk like your father and get in the game, comprende."

"$25.00 per."

He smiled, "that's a start." Before I could answer with another offer, he changed gears on me.

"After he said my name, he fell asleep and left me sitting there, thinking as hard as I could. I don't know how long it was I sat there, before I realized Gem had left the wagon and was walking toward me. She looked different. The little smile was the same, her walk was the same. Her hair was the same bright red, although it had grown out and she had a lot of it. Gem didn't look like a boy anymore. She didn't look like Felicity Brown or one of the dainty birds; I don't mean that. She just didn't look like the little kid that shot at Rufus Waggoner up in Kansas. She was pretty.

I got up from the man on the ground and said, "let us go check the livestock." We got quite a ways from the barn before I spoke. "Could you hear us talking from inside the wagon?"

"No, not really, but I wasn't trying. Why, you think he heard us talking about Felicity's money?"

"Maybe he did, his eyes were open when I came out of the wagon."

"That might not be the best thing for us?"

"Sit down; there's more. That man is a special deputy voted on and hired by the city of Lawrence Kansas to hunt you and me down. He killed those two boys I just buried because one of them rode a black horse. One of them was shot in the back."

"You don't think he suspects us, do you?"

"There is one more detail I have not yet shared; he knows my name." "I think we should be safe. He is looking for two boys and he apparently thinks he has sent them on their way to the pearly gates."

"If he knows my name and about the horse, do you think it would stand to reason he knows about my father's sword?"

"Yes, I do."

"Shit!"

" We can hide it with the two rifles we found; I think it will fit in there."

"Good idea, Gem. If he were to find the sword, or the weapons, or the bag of money. The portrait that would paint would probably not be hanging up in any southern court house. That would be us hanging there from the nearest tree."

"Speaking of the pearly gates."

The sword fit in the hiding place along with the rifles. We both agreed that was a much better place for it anyway.

The next couple of days were pleasant and restful for everything, horses, mules, shot up deputies, and me and Gem. We found some lime and made up enough white wash to paint the wagon covering up Felicity Brown's sign on both sides. Before we painted there was some discussion on the pros and cons of erasing the final trace of Felicity Brown's time on earth.

Thinking and talking about her made us a little melancholy and a little happy at the same time.

Gem more so than me.

We decided, given all the circumstances, Felicity probably would be happy to see her wagon in our hands. Had she experienced a different outcome on that fateful day, she might have not felt quite so charitable. We laughed at that. Gem and I both agreed it didn't matter much. She being in the better place and all.

The outside of the wagon looked entirely different after the paint job. New paint would not erase the memory of Felicity, and that was alright, it was not our goal. We did not want it to.

Things like that take time.

The deputy seemed to be getting better. Gem made up some kind of broth he could get down and his color was coming back.

GEM

One morning standing at the fence on the other side of our horses were two horses that had come in from somewhere. They were saddled and bridled, the bay horse had his saddle rolled under his belly. The other one's saddle was still in place. They were both dragging their reins, although one of them on the bay was snapped off. He must have stepped on it or something. The one with the saddle in the right place was black with two white hooves on the front.

If these two horses belonged to the two boys I buried, and I knew they did. The 'special deputy' had apparently murdered those two boys for riding a black horse that did not match the description he had been given and passed on to me. The horse that did match the description was standing next to me about twenty feet from the wounded man. My blood ran cold, I was scared.

I let the horses in with the others, unsaddled them and walked to the barn. I needed to talk to Gem. It was dark in the barn and it took a moment for my eyes to adjust. When they did I realized the deputy was leaning against the wagon with a pistol pointed at Gem.

"I heard you and that boy talking about the money hid in the wagon and I want it!"

I gave no thought to my actions, I yelled and charged that man with all my might. He turned to see about the commotion I was making, exposing his wounded side. I drove my shoulder into him and that wound so hard it knocked me down. He continued to turn around like I was nothing more than a mosquito bite and put the pistol on me. And cocked the hammer. I didn't like one single thing about that man, but I had to admire his pure toughness.

His eyes were blank and cold with no light in them. He simply stared at me and didn't blink, once.

"Like I told that girl, I want the money in the wagon."

"There's no money in there."

"Shut the hell up boy, I'll kill you where you lay, and I'll have my way with her, before I kill her. I know about the money."

I believed him. "She will need help." I started to get up.

"Be gentle boy, in how you move."

I was.

He motioned toward the wagon door with the hand that held the pistol, "slow." That was my chance and I jumped at it and him. The moment I banged into him, Gem hit him in the head with the coffee pot. He dropped the pistol and slowly sat down.

Gem had not only cold cocked him, she had left him covered in coffee grounds.

I picked up his gun and put the barrel to his head.

"I don't know, Davey."

"What's not to know Gem, his intention was mayhem and death for us!"

"That is completely true, I know."

"He killed those two boys, I think to simply rob them of their horses."

"After the bold actions he displayed against us, I'm sure that is true. But to put a hole in his brain pan as he lays there helpless, I don't know."

"Gem."

"In the heat of battle or in defense of our selves I would not blink an eye. However, this is execution, this is murder. Can you live with that?"

"Yes, I can."

"Alright get me a pistol, we will both shoot him at the same time."

"What are you sayin Gem?"

"What I'm telling you, is to do it like this is wrong and it will haunt you. This man deserves to die. I can't and won't argue that. If you think this has to be done, we will do it together and live with the consequences together."

"Gem I can't ask you for that."

"You ain't askin me, I'm tellin you that's how it's going to be."

In the end we hooked up the wagon and left him alive.

Gem made sure the broth was within reach when he came to and I put the bay horse inside the fence and took the black with us.

I did not particularly care if he lived, but because of Gems good heart he had a better chance than he would have given us.

Of course, our thinking was all wrong. We made about ten, twelve miles that day and didn't give much thought to our decisions about the deputy.

Gem and I both had seen and heard of southern partisans wounded and left by a creek or out back of someone's farm to heal up or die.

Armies had doctors and medical help. None of us were in the army and we all knew our fate if shot. Having doctored Gem in the woods, we knew first hand.

Maybe some of his Redleg pals would find him, maybe they wouldn't.

There was a lot of war still going where we were headed.

Gem didn't think a lot of that and truth be known I was not partial to it much myself. Things were pretty much as they had been before we split off from Quantrill, only now we weren't working for anyone. Our spying days, I guess, had run their course. Some days we got stopped by soldiers in blue, some days the soldiers wore grey. We saw no more Redlegs. The roads were still filled with people that had nowhere to go and not much of anything to eat.

One day we stopped to talk to an old man and some people to find out where we were. Over off the road were some raggedy lookin little kids playing on a mound of dirt. I thought at least the children were alright. Then I realized they were playing with a skull and some bones of a dead soldier.

They said we were close to Carthage and it had been bad there but seemed quiet now.

The old man put his hand up on the wagon seat, looked at us with watery eyes and said. "Watch for the Home Guard they are the bad players in this part of the country. They'd as soon kill and rob as talk. Strike with no warning, shoot you and have their fun with your little missy there."

They hollered at the kids playing on the mound of dirt and started up the road in the opposite direction as us. I got the feeling they had nowhere to go.

"Little missy he said, you heard him." Gem beamed.

I remember thinkin', *are we better off now or when she looked like a boy?*

"Is have their fun, like what it was with the dainty birds?" "I always thought the dainty birds enjoyed what they were doing. I think the way that man said it, with these men, not too much of it involved joy."

Everything was tore up. Any house or barn we could see was burned and ruined, all the fences were down, and the fields looked like craters on the moon.

The old man was right the war was here. Somehow without a mark or scratch on it was a sign that said Carthage 5 miles and about 50 feet from the sign were two men sitting on their horses passing a bottle back and forth.

"I don't think they've seen us yet. Keep on going, I'll get the pistol." I jumped in the back and Gem drove on toward the men. We were on them almost before they knew it.

The two men were drunk, drunk so bad to sit a horse seemed impossible. One of them said something that sounded like stand and deliver, the other one got out his pistol. Gem stopped, they just stared like they could no longer speak English.

"What do you two want, will you give me the road?"

That got um talking.

"Don't use an uppity tone with us girly, we represent the law. We are the home guard."

"As far as I can see you look like a couple of drunks, why aren't you off fighting for the cause?"

"We are the law."

"Oh, I see, you are the law."

"And it will be in your best interest to keep that thought fresh in your mind."

"If I may ask, what might the law be doing out here by the side of the road drinking whiskey in the middle of the day?"

I didn't know if they were that drunk or just plain stupid.

"Why ma'am we are posted here to look for these two desperados." And he held up the wanted poster of me and Gem.

"I understand them to be southern men are you two not the same?"

"Yes, ma'am we are, but look at the money that's offered." While they were using what little vocabulary, they had at their disposal to explain their version of the way things were in their county, I eased out the back of the wagon. Standing behind them I cocked the hammer and said, "Do not turn around and do drop the weapons and do get off those horses." They did.

Gem looked down at them, "Do I look like one of those boys in that poster you dumb crackers?"

"No ma'am, no ma'am you sure don't ma'am."

"Then get." She pointed back the way we came. "If you stop and look around for one instant, that will be your last instant, understand!"

"Yes ma'am." The one that did the talking was still holding the bottle. "Can we take this?"

"Yes, you can take your whiskey."

By the way Gem said it I could tell she was more disgusted than scared of the two home guard men.

"They lost their horses and their dignity to a couple of kids in a wagon but saved the whiskey. What do you think about that?"

"It must be some powerful stuff."

"I think you are right, I doubt I will ever have much familiarity with it. It doesn't appear to give out a favorable result."

"She never did, I on the other hand found it enjoyable."

Mr. Richards laughed, Maggie didn't.

"Where are we on the horse negotiations Benny, I have kind of forgotten?"

"You seemed interested in my offer of fifteen dollars per."

"Well played Benny. You could have a future in horse trading yet. Correct me if I'm wrong, I think I seemed interested in my offer of thirty-five dollars per horse."

That old man had just played me like a violin and we both knew it.

"We can talk about our horse deal tomorrow." He let me off the hook.

Chapter XVI

Gem and I talked it over and decided it might not be too good an idea to ride into town with the two horses we had inherited from the drunks. Maybe they were telling it straight about representing the law and they probably were. Someone in town was in charge and it stood to reason they were smarter than the two at the sign.

We left the saddles in the middle of the road. Gem figured the two addlebrained derelicts trying to pass themselves off as law enforcement men would not want to leave behind the saddles, they had no doubt stolen off some poor downtrodden pilgrims.

A couple miles from town we turned their horses loose. They followed us for a little while but soon lost interest in favor of the green grass by the side of the road.

Just this side of town was a good place to camp, with plenty of grass and a creek.

"Davey what are we going to do about the wanted posters?"

"They are bothersome true, however they are looking for two boys."

"It might be time to quit Felicity's wagon."

"Why?"

"The special deputy knows about it, those two drunken pea brains know about it. I told the union major the wagon belonged to my dead grandmother."

"I'm not sure I'm following?"

"They all had the poster in common."

"You think that's a stretch, what's the chance of them getting into the same place and talking about the two of us?"

"Slim, I admit. I think we can move and be out of this part of the country a lot faster on horse back."

"Well, that does make some sense."

"Some sense!"

"I guess you are right it does make sense."

"Damn right Davey, after all in the eyes of the world we are no good Missouri bushwhackers with a price on our head."

"You are a funny girl, Gem."

"I don't know about funny, I want to be gone from all this. Those two drunks scared me. We are two ducks in a pond sitting on that wagon. I say burn it. We have everything we need to move more freely through the country side."

She was right we had four horses, two mules, two rifles, I don't know how many pistols, a satchel full of money, and a sword.

Gem looked at me in a way new to me. "Do we agree?"

Even if I didn't, I wouldn't have said so.

The next morning, we burned the wagon and tied our plunder on the mules as best we could and rode into town looking like a couple of farm kid refugees and rode out looking like we owned a freight company. Even after we bought supplies, packsaddles, ammunition and new things for us to wear, we had not put a dent in Felicity's money.

Gem and I decided, as best we could, she should look like a boy still. Up close that would not work anymore, but from a ways off it might. We thought new hats with broad brims might cover our faces some and make us look older. Gem put a feather in the band on her hat. A big one, kind of Quantrill style. I wasn't so sure about the feather, but she was.

We also decided not to hide our weapons any more. We wanted no trouble, but if it came our way and it would, we would be better enabled to deal with it. I wore two pistols around my waist and two mounted on the saddle. I tried to figure a way to strap on my father's sword.

Gem found that to be the most comical thing she had ever seen. I thought I looked rather knight-errant, a swashbuckler, a man of action. It ended up wrapped in canvas and tied on one of the mules.

Gem carried one on her person and two on her saddle. That seems excessive now, still we had more or less grown up with Missouri border ruffians and that's what we knew. All the arma'ament in the world would be no help if we got stopped by federals. It was the home guard or bounty hunters that we were thinking of.

Headed south out of town the federal soldiers were working on the telegraph line. They paid us no mind, even though on some of the poles wanted posters of us were tacked on in amongst the other flyers and advertisements.

Felicity's wagon had benefits that's true and we missed some of them. Traveling by horse was safer and quicker. It only took three days to reach Fort Smith and we had no trouble or adventures.

Fort Smith at that time was under union control, sort of. They held the town but that was pretty much all they had under control. Rebel armies were all around the country side and attacks happened often.

Just inside the city limits, a corporal with a federal patrol had some questions that he felt Gem and I could provide the answers to. "That's a nice looking outfit you two fellows have there. Where did it come from? You are well armed and well mounted. I think maybe we should take you to headquarters and have the captain talk to you. What do you think?"

"Well sir."

"I am a corporal, boy, not a sir."

"I meant no offense corporal."

"State your business."

"We are freighters by trade, sir, I mean corporal. We hauled freight up in Kansas until those filthy southern guerrillas left us orphaned."

"Why are you two here?"

"Here, sir?"

"Fort Smith not in Kansas?"

"We heard there was work for freighters here."

"That could be true I wouldn't know much about freighting. Head in that direction and turn left at the second street, that's where the freighters congregate."

"Thank you, we will."

The corporal came close and held the bridle on my horse. He and his horse did not move.

My heart stood still, there was no way to win in a pistol fight or out run the soldiers. He looked me right in the eye. "You ever given any thought to signing up and fighting for your country?"

"Yes, sir I have, to join the union army I have to wait another year. I am too young."

"We can find ways to get around the age part."

"No corporal, I want to do it right. I'll wait, thank you though." He let go of the bridle and we rode away.

"You ought to be selling women's under garments, as full of shit as you are."

The freight office was where the corporal said, and we rode up. There were horses and mules and teamsters milling around everywhere. In back surrounded by a fence were supplies in every shape, size, and description. Tacked to the wall by the door was our wanted poster. A man standing there saw me looking at it.

"A guy would stand to make some real money if he found those two traitorous Missouri snakes."

On the other side of the door a man said. "You blue coat loving pig, those two are heroes!"

The first man walked over to the second man. "Sir I have a distinctly different opinion of what is the right of this."

The second man never said a word of any kind. He simply hit the first man full in the face and made his nose bleed. In the blink of an eye those two were rolling around in the dirt and a couple of other fellows had jumped in and started beatin on each other.

I couldn't tell one from the other. A big man with a vest and a gold chain stepped out the door and fired a shotgun in the air. "Quit!" The shotgun blast got their full and undivided attention. "Take it down the road."

Even though they did, I got the distinct impression those four were far from being done.

He looked over at us. "Mike Murphy is my name, mostly I answer to and you can call me Murphy. How can I be of service to you two?"

GEM

The closer we got, the bigger he got. He looked to me to be about six foot four or five and I would guess around two forty or fifty well muscled pounds. The big Mexican hat he wore added to his size. He didn't look like the kind to trifle with.

"We would like to haul freight for you."

"It's rare we hire girls."

"I can pull my own weight, Murphy." Gem gave the man her hardest look.

Murphy gave Gem a hard look and said. "Tell you what I'm going to do little miss. Your partner and I are going back into my office and when he come out if you still have this nice brand new outfit of yours, I will hire both of you. Deal."

"Deal."

His office was dark and cool inside. "Here is my offer to you. I will supply the loads and lease you ten mules for twenty Yankee dollars, payable at the end of the trip. I think that's fair. You think that's fair?"

I nodded. "Yes, sir that seems fair, I will take you at your word."

"I will give you twenty per cent of the profit on your loads when we get there. We go in a caravan and I will supply the cook and the grub."

"Sir may I ask the destination?"

"Whys that?"

"I think that is a logical question."

"You do?"

"I do."

"Texas through the Indian nations. It is away, for the most part, from the war. Still I would not try to pass this off as some sort of cake walk. There will be danger and that little girl out there will be smack dab in the middle of it. You alright with that?"

Again, I nodded.

"The men are rough but fair and will treat the girl alright, I think. On the trail there will be no drinking, gambling or talk of who is right or wrong in the war. The cook and his brother go by the names Mathew and Mark. Their mother may have been pious and reverent, the sons not so much. Those two men at great risk to their own life saved me when I got into some trouble up in Virginia. Those are two of the most honorable men I have ever known, and they are blacker than the ace of spades and free men. You have a problem with that?"

"No sir, I don't." I thought maybe he would expand on 'some trouble in Virginia'. Instead he offered his hand, it was huge, and I took it.

"Put your live stock in pen number four and keep a close eye on them until after we leave. It will be a different set of thieves after them, when we leave here."

"Thank you, sir we will not let you down."

"If you do, I'll leave you right where it happens, make no mistake."

"Well, Gem we are mule skinners."

"Can we pull it off?"

"We better, sounds to me like it will be a long walk back if we don't."

"Davey those men were fighting over you and me."

"Think we should have said something?"

"No, I do not, besides what in God's name could we possibly say?"

"One side thinks we did some good, the other not so much. I hope all this simply goes away."

"Me too, but I don't think it's going too."

"Where are we to put our livestock until we leave?"

Chapter XVII

"That man Murphy will be our boss and he laid out what appeared to be a reasonable deal for us to exit this part of the world. I wish you'd been in the office with me, to help with the fine points."

"You did fine."

"I guess we'll find out. He has a place for us behind the office." The pen turned out fine and right across from it was a boarding house with a small place to eat. I unsaddled and looked to the stock. Gem went over to the boarding house to get us something to eat.

We had decided at least one of us had to stay with the stock at all times. Then, of course, there was Felicity's money. There was more danger in it than getting the horses stole. The pack saddles we bought were made with big pockets to stuff with hay or straw between the load and the saddle pad, to protect the animals back.

I put some of Felicity's money in the bottom of each pocket and packed the hay on top.

We knew it would not stand much scrutiny but reasoned no one would have any idea of us being the rich orphans we were and wouldn't think to look too close.

When Gem returned it was a choice between bacon and eggs or a week-old newspaper. The bacon won.

Gem told me the boarding house would take either Yankee greenbacks or Confederate money. It cost two and a half times more to use Confederate.

"Davey," Gem started. "Davey there is a picture taker over there at the boarding house, you think we should have our likeness made?"

This was, of course, one of those there is no debate sort of questions. Gem took back the dishes, set a time with the photographer and I started in on the newspaper.

On the back of the second page was an article about the infamous "Lawrence Assassins". Come to find out, Gem and I had murdered two more high ranking union officers. This time on the outskirts of Leavenworth, Kansas and it was widely suspected that we were involved in three other shootings in Missouri and one in Kentucky. The article went on to say the Kansas legislation was working on a bill to raise enough money to generate interest with the Pinkerton Detective Agency in taking on the case. The newspaper reported my name as Richard Davies and had yet to find a name for the other assassin. From what the reporter could glean from the many eye witnesses, the other low life shooter was described as short in stature and had eyes that not only were two different colors {one blue one brown} they showed the craziness and obvious mental deficiency exhibited by most southern fighters.

"Aren't we something?"

"They got you described to a T, Gem."

"Do you need to be writing my obituary? I'm sure I am a gone goose and this carefree life as a bushwhacker is close to drawing to an end."

"Gem it is funny now, I wonder what will happen when one of those newspaper men get it right?"

"The Pacific Ocean."

"The Pacific Ocean?"

"Remember right after Felicity died and those fellows you knew stopped us on the road?"

"The James brothers"? "Remember we told that Yankee officer that was the destination we had in mind?"

"I think I have a stronger memory of sitting under a wanted poster in that man's office."

"Davey, we have already signed on for Texas, how much farther could the Pacific Ocean be?"

"I guessin, but it couldn't be all that far. I'm in if you are. Let's set our sights on Texas first, you think?"

"They wear grass skirts there, I read that."

"Dresses made of grass, I don't think that's true Gem."

"Well, I believe it to be the case and I also believe you and I both know how we will solve this little mystery of ours." It was plain to see I had voiced the wrong opinion and Gem was not happy about it and that I held no winning cards in this conversation.

Later that day Gem told me she was sorry for being cranky and in ill spirits. She had dreamed of her mother and a horrible sense of melancholy she couldn't shake.

I found no fault with that, we had lost parents in common.

"Davey, I told Quantrill and those others that found me, my plight was a result of Kansas Redlegs. That was not the whole story. There were some Redlegs, but it was mainly regular union army soldiers.

I have no memory of my father, he died or left us right after I was born. My mother really never said. We did alright, the two of us, even prospered some. Until she got sick and was not able to work. She was a seamstress of some repute, at least in our area.

We lived, and mother worked in a small cottage behind the main house on the Russell plantation. It was a grand place, all the fences and buildings were painted white, with dark blue trim on the house. The grounds surrounding it were kept in tip top shape, so green it made your eyes water. They raised cotton and some tobacco and treated their slaves with tolerance.

Mister Russell joined up early and went to Virginia. I think he was a major or maybe higher. It don't matter, he died almost as quick as he left. Mrs. Russell never knew where or how, just that he was dead.

I watched as mother got sicker and sicker, I knew she was filled with pain. She would sometimes cry and tell me about her fear of death or ask what would become of me, her fine baby girl. Mostly though she stared at the ceiling and waited.

Mrs. Russell was a saint to me, no finer person ever lived. She saw to it I got some education and was being raised according to the values and morals of good southern women.

One cold and cloudy night we heard the soldiers come up our road. The officer ordered everyone to stand in front of the main house and watch just exactly what happens to rebel lovers.

We all stood there shivering and watched.

I watched when some of the soldiers got off their horses and set fire to the place. I cried out please, please stop. I pointed at the little cottage my mother and I lived in and told the man in charge, a short ugly man with a nose swollen and pocked marked from whiskey, my mother was sick in there. I watched him order two of his men to drag her out. I watched when they set fire to the little house. I watched as Mrs. Russell stood over my mother, in silent defiance.

The same officer that previously had ordered his men drag my mother out of the house, now ordered the same two men to open fire on Mrs. Russell. I watched Mrs. Russell fall.

The soldiers gathered up everything they could carry and herded the livestock and slaves down the road and never looked back

If they had looked back, they would have seen a little girl named Precious Gem holding her dying mother on the ground next to the body of Mrs. Russell. Davey, there was not one thing, not one single thing I could do for my mother. I sat there for two days and nights and held her.

Then it started to rain, hard. Still I cradled Mother on my lap. When the rain stopped, I realized she was gone, into the welcoming arms of Jesus. There was nothing I could do, I just got up and walked away."

I could only look at her, I did not possess the vocabulary or the ability to convey my feelings of sorrow and horror at what that poor girl had suffered.

I walked over and put my arms around her. She cried.

Mr. Richards stopped his narrative and pointed at Maggie. Maggie wasn't making a sound, her face was pale and tears were streaming down her face.

"Benny that's enough for today, go get the pickup."

Gladly, if I stayed a minute longer, I'd be bawling too. I thought about the old tin type on the shelf in the living room. Those two young faces had seen more of the worst side of life, than I could ever imagine.

Chapter XVIII

M r. Richards wanted to drive down to the feed store and see to some things, which I took as he wanted out of the house and to talk with some of his friends. I found two reasons to agree and one of them was Jeanie. Jeanie wasn't there.

Actually, it was alright she wasn't, I enjoyed my time with Mr. Richards pals. For the first time in my life the men talked to me like I was an equal, not some kid hanging around.

A couple of Mr. Richards's friends made a point of telling me what a good job I was doing, taking care of Davey's ranch. One of them actually shook my hand.

Mister Richards and I pissed away most of the afternoon bullshittin with who ever came by. The different men talked about current cattle prices and told stories involving horses both good and bad. We talked about Roosevelt and the pros and cons of the new deal.

For the first time I heard about Germany and what they were doing in Europe. It didn't sound good, but Germany was a long way from northern California.

I was getting a little worried about wearing him out and setting him back, but he was having so much fun visiting I didn't say anything.

Maggie wasn't going to be pleased with me.

On two different occasions I heard the story of me and the cows and the drunk on the highway. Other than me in them, both stories didn't have much in common with how I remembered it taking place.

Finally, Mr. Richards asked me if I would please take him home, he said he had had enough for today. We got in the pick up and started for the ranch.

"Benny, you figure out our horse deal yet?" I was all set to toss another offer his way, but he had already fallen asleep.

When we got to the ranch he got out of the pickup and went straight to bed without mentioning anything about the horses. I understood why of course, he was still pretty sick and putting all that aside he was the oldest person I had ever encountered in my life. It stood to reason Maggie was not going to be pleased with me. I was dreading our next conversation.

Maggie came out of Mr. Richards's room under a full head of steam. I just stood there waiting, wondering if she was going to yell at me or beat the living shit out of me. She grabbed me and pulled me into those enormous bosoms of hers.

"Benny thank you, thank you, I think you brought that old man back to life."

"I don't know what I did?"

"Even, God forbid, he dies tonight he will die a happy man."

He didn't.

When I got up the next morning Mr. Richards was outside building a fire. "Ben thank you for taking me to town yesterday. I meant to work on our horse deal. It is my fault we did not get it accomplished. I promise we will get it done. I know it is important to your father."

"That's ok, I know we will."

"Benny you ever have sourdough biscuits made in a Dutch oven?"

"No sir, can't say as I have?"

"Well boy you are in for a treat, if I can remember how to build em. It has been awhile. Dutch ovens have been around two or three hundred years, hell they came over with the pilgrims. In this modern age not so, many people know how or even care to learn the art of the Dutch. Basco sheepherders still use them and hunters and people like that. I don't think it looms large in the world of electricity or in the lives of enlightened cooks and why should it? Feeding people is hard work and every little thing helps

When we went to work for Murphy our job was to pack the Dutch ovens, not the ones the cooks used. The ones we hauled were brand new. He bought them in Fort Smith for two dollars, Yankee, and sold them in Texas for twenty. A twelve-inch Dutch weighs about twenty pounds. Murphy had special pack boxes made that held five. That adds up to ten per mule times ten mules. Remember he paid two dollars and sold them for twenty.

When we first started it took Gem and I together to load the mules, but it wasn't all that long before we could each do it by ourselves. Murphy liked that."

The fire was getting close to being burned down to the coals, not quite but close.

"Mathew was a master at cooking with these type ovens and Mark was no piker either.

Gem and I watched and learned. Mark wasn't talkative or outgoing especially around Gem. I don't know if it was because she was a girl or a white girl or maybe both. When I asked something he generally answered. When Gem would ask something generally he did not, he would cast his eyes down and walk away.

Mathew took life pretty seriously. Mark did not. He would say things like God came to him in a dream and, you are one lucky sombitch. You are going to get to cook for a bunch of white folks. Or he might say something to the affect, if you go around smelling skunk's, assholes all day pretty soon good company will be hard to find.

Once he walked up to me and out of the clear blue sky and said, everybody knows never ask a barber if you need a haircut. Is he morally obligated to tell you the true condition of your hair or is he morally obligated to earn a living?

At first, I thought God Damn, that's about the dumbest human I have ever been around. It took me awhile before I came to realize just how smart that man was. There have been few people in my life, that when we finished our conversion and I walked away. I could not stop thinking about the things he said, sometimes for days.

They were good men, I heard they got themselves killed somewhere down by the Red River a few years later. I don't know if that's true or not, I hope not. Like I said they were good men.

Without going into great detail on how he did it, other than to tell me the secret to cooking biscuits was very little heat on the bottom and most of the heat on the top of the oven.

I guess he remembered, the biscuits were great.

Mr. Richards had one, Maggie had one and yours truly ate the rest. Then and there I knew that was a skill I needed to learn.

"I'm kinda getting ahead of the story. It took some time for Murphy to put together all the parts and pieces in his caravan. Diverse would be putting it mildly.

There were ex-soldiers from both sides. Some of the southern men had taken their parole and were not on active duty any more. Some were former union soldiers. There were deserters from both armies'. A few of them were still in the Confederate army and serving under Murphy.

Gem was convinced that a combination like that would prove volatile. But for the most part the various groups got on pretty well. In no small part due to Murphy's leadership, his was a tight ship.

Being from the part of the country I came from I had no real experience with Mexicans or even Texans for that matter. I came to think more of the Mexicans. Their way of handling horses and livestock became the foundation of everything I did with stock.

I held a low opinion of Quakers because of their aligning with Kansas Redlegs in the Missouri border conflicts and there were a whole gaggle of them trying to sign up with Murphy.

Then there were the people trying to escape the war. Families with children of all ages and sizes. People with a lot of belongings, people with no belongings. Some had oxen or mules to pull their wagons. Some rode horses and some intended to walk.

Gem wondered if it was becoming something biblical, I thought it was anything but that.

Whatever it was, it was going on all around where Gem and I were staying.

Gem and I split up the guard duty and didn't get much sleep trying to keep track of our horses and tack.

Even with our best vigilance in place someone snuck in the pen and stole my father's horse, Lord Nelson."

Mr. Richards looked me in the eye, shook his head and said, "Believe me Benny when I tell you the irony of that was not lost on Gem and me."

"Nothing else was gone not even the pack saddles with Felicity Browns money. I spent all the next day looking for the horse, to no avail.

Gem thought it might be a good idea to ask Murphy if he had thoughts on who might have or where might have the horse gone. Seemed a good idea.

Murphy's office was closed up tight, when I got there. The saloon across the street was open and that's where I found him, bellied up to the bar. He was talking to a rough dressed man that looked small standing next to Murphy. Murphy was so big everybody looked little. The man wasn't little. Murphy saw me standing by the door and waved me over.

"Davey come in and meet an old friend of mine." I walked over and stood in front of the two men.

If it wasn't for the other men in the bar, I might have thought I had become a pigmy in the time it took for me to walk over. Those two men were big.

"Davey Richards meet Charles Goodnight a cowman from Texas." "Davey this old fallen from grace southern gentleman tells me you and some little slip of a girl have signed on with him to go to Texas."

"Yes sir, that's the game we want to play." I tried to sound tough. However, by the way they

155

looked at each other I don't think I was very persuasive.

'When you have enough of Murphy's bullshit, look me up. I aim to trail a herd of cattle up north. After this God Damned war is over."

Murphy finished his drink and ordered three more. "How's something like that work?"

The bar tender never said a word when he handed me the whiskey. I didn't say anything either.

The three of us turned away from the bar and Goodnight started talking.

"Ranching in Texas is in shambles and there are thousands and thousands of longhorn cattle free for the taking. The demand for beef in the east will be huge."

"You planning on driving them to New York?" I asked.

"That's a smart kid, Murphy. No, the railroad is as close as Kansas." "Kansas, Kansas I just left that part of the country. Those filthy God forsaken low life Kansas Redlegs kill you all and steal your cows." Oh shit, I just made the kind of statement that stood a good chance of getting me killed.

"Jesus kid keep your voice down." Murphy and Goodnight both turned me back facing the bar. "Maybe you are not as smart as I thought."

"No." Murphy said. "This kid, and that girl he's with, are smart. Charlie finish that drink and meet me and the kid at my office."

Murphy grabbed me by the collar and steered me out of the bar and across the street to his office. I'm not sure my feet touched the ground. It was dark and stuffy in the office. "Don't ever talk like that in public, you understand!"

"Yes sir, I do, I know better."

Murphy opened a desk drawer pulled out a horse pistol and walked to the window. Parting the curtains, he looked out. "You know Felicity Brown?"

Before I could answer Goodnight came in and quickly closed the door, moved over to the other window and pulled the pistol from his holster. They stood there for what seemed the longest time, then relaxed and looked at me.

Goodnight asked me if I wanted a pull off the bottle.

"No sir, not at this time, but thank you." I can't say what the fastest thing on earth is. I can say whatever it might be, it is slower than the speed I was asking my brain to work at that moment.

"You were looking for me?" Murphy sat back at his desk but didn't put the pistol back in the drawer.

"Yes sir, one of my horses has gone missing."

"The good looking black with the white sock on the hind."

I just looked at him. "How'd you know that?"

He smiled. "There is a lot I know, now tell me if you know Felicity Brown."

"Yes sir, I did." I was hoping that might end the conversation, it didn't

"Did?"

I had to make a choice, if I was wrong I knew what would happen to me. I did not care to offer up the same fate for Gem. "Sir she has passed."

"Passed, you mean to tell me she is dead?" Murphy took his hat off and leaned back in the chair. For the briefest moment I saw what I took to be pain in his eyes. Then it was back to business.

"Yes sir, I am sorry to say it is true."

"You better start talkin boy and now would be the best time to start!"

"Southern border ruffians shot her off the wagon seat. Gem was sitting right beside her."

"Where were you while this was going on?"

"On a scout about three quarters of a mile away."

Goodnight jumped in. "On a scout you say?"

"Yes sir, Felicity would send one of us, by that I mean me or Gem, ahead to scout up customers for her dainty birds."

Both men looked at each other and smiled, they knew Felicity and the dainty birds.

"Describe the events of her death."

Now it might be getting sticky. "The one son of a bitch rode out of the trees with his buddies close behind. He said something to Felicity, I guess he did not agree with her response and killed her right then and there. No sooner had the sound of his shot faded away, when a bunch of Federals came out of the opposite side in the woods and dispatched the black hearted bastards."

"That's quite the tale."

"Yes sir."

"How did it come to be, you were there with Felicity?"

Now the fat was in the fire, I took a drink of the whiskey to stall for some time and instantly was sorry. Whiskey is an acquired taste. I did acquire it, but not at that moment.

"Sir if I may inquire, what if anything was Felicity and the dainty birds to you two. I mean no disrespect at all, but there are certain aspects of her life that maybe ought not to be shared."

Goodnight moved his hand down to his holster. "Share!"

Murphy looked over at Goodnight. "The kid's right, he don't really know us and how he should answer."

Goodnight relaxed and said, "Kid if you live through this war you'd be missing a bet if you don't run for governor, you are a born politician."

He turned to Murphy, "See you in Texas, I need to be getting in the wind." Then he looked at me. "Think my offer over." He went out the door, forked his horse and was gone, as far as I knew, back to Texas.

Chapter XIX

I t seemed like the life in the room left with him, but only for a short time. Murphy started in. "I was born and raised in Virginia and Felicity Brown was my mother's best friend and mother to a boy and two girls. She was truly a gentle soul and kind hearted woman. When the war started I joined up first thing and was made a captain in General Lee's Army of Northern Virginia. I was in the thick of things for about a year before I got hit." He smiled and shrugged his shoulders. "General Lee assigned Mathew and Mark to smuggle me back home to heal up. The Yankees held most of my home country by then and to say the trip home was not without adventure would be putting it mildly.

When I got home everything was different, by that I mean Yankees and Marshall Law everywhere. Felicity Brown's boy had been shot down in front of her and the girls. When she got past the worst of her grief she went to work for the cause.

My mother took in the two girls. I spent two months hiding up a side hill in the back of a canyon quite a way from town.

The two sisters rigged up a canvas lean to for me by a small creek. The two girls took turns slipping past the enemy lines to bring me food and help clean my wounds.

When my wounds quit hurting, I tracked down the General and reported back for duty. He had a different plan for me than I figured. The Confederacy thought Texas was going to be very important to the Federals. My orders were to help with the plan to get all the weapons into Texas as humanly possible."

I interrupted "You're a captain in the Confederacy?"

"Yes, but I'm not a captain anymore I'm a major and every once in a while, they send me a paycheck."

I don't know, maybe I was getting hard to convince. I wanted to trust him. I wished Gem was here. Murphy, I think, kinda sensed what was going on in my brain. "A couple of days ago a fellow stopped in my office. Told me a big windy about being a special deputy from Lawrence Kansas with a mandate to find two wanted killers from up there. Know anything about that?"

I just looked at him.

"Said they killed the Governor in cold blood, shot him in the back, in the dead of night."

I wondered if Murphy could see the sweat forming up by my hatband.

"Said these two lowlifes stole the governor's prize racehorse. A black with one white sock."

"That was my father's horse." I knew I should keep my mouth shut but I couldn't. Enough is enough.

"Your father's horse you say?"

Maybe I'm being melodramatic, maybe I'm not, but I just roped the grizzly bear and there was no backin up now.

"Yes sir, Lord Nelson was the pride of my father's horse herd."

"Speakin of big windys, you gonna sit there and tell me a fella with a badge from Lawrence Kansas is makin up a tale like that? How's something like that work, enlighten me. Please."

"Sir I'm not sure where to begin."

"How bout at the beginning."

"My father was a Bengal Lancer and we had a horse farm in Missouri."

"Into the valley of death rode the six hundred?"

"Yes sir."

"You figure I'm some sort of poor willing pilgrim, that'll believe any sort of tale laid at my feet?"

"I can prove it."

"You can prove a horse stole out of Kansas belongs to your father?"

"No sir, I can prove my father was one of Prince Alberts own."

"What's your father's take on this story going to be?"

"Sir, my father speaks no longer."

"And my young sir, why is that?"

"God Damned Kansas Redlegs is why that is!" I was pissed now, and I let out the whole story. How I found my father, how Quantrill found me, how Frank James gave me a pistol with blood on it. I told him how George Todd and Quantrill conspired to pawn Gem off on me. Then I told him how Gem and I became the infamous child assassins the papers keep writing about. I included the part about Gem getting shot and hiding out in the woods. It used up the better part of an hour to tell Murphy the story, he never said a word the entire time. When I finished, he said, "Goodnight has your father's horse."

"Goodnight stole him?"

Murphy found that idea funny. "No, I told him to take the horse. You will get him back on down the trail."

"With all due respect sir why in the God damned world would you take it upon yourself to give my horse to someone else for safekeeping?" He had lit the fuse on my temper and I needed to do something. What that was I didn't know. To say I was mad was to sugar coat the way I was feeling toward Murphy. Maybe not so much Murphy as everything about my life and the world I lived in. And I knew there was nothing I could do.

"Cool down kid, I knew who you two were from the second day you were here in town.

"Why make me tell my tale, then?"

"I coulda been wrong."

"I know who the man with the badge is, the one huntin me and Gem. I buried two of his mistakes. One of them got it in the back. Gem patched him up and his way of saying thank you was to try to rob us of Felicity's wagon. Gem bless her heart, cold cocked him with a coffee pot. I wanted to kill him where he lay. Gem pointed it out to me that murder was not a trait she admired. We left him there with some food and water and one of Felicity's blankets."

"What became of Felicity's wagon and her things?"

"We burned the wagon and in the way of valuables there wasn't much. Some money, some guns and a letter from General Lee."

"You can keep the money and the guns. I don't care, I would like to see the letter from Marse Lee."

"I'll give you the letter when I get my horse back." When I said that Murphy looked down at his pistol laying there on the desk where he had set it earlier. Very slowly he reached down and picked it up.

I figured my goose was cooked.

He smiled and put the pistol back in the drawer.

I gave him the letter later that day.

He got kind of emotional and thanked me and said he would always cherish it and thanked me one more time.

I think I saw Lord Nelson again, but I can't be sure, there was a lot going on that day. The next morning, I got up early and left Gem sleeping peacefully. My plan was to bring her breakfast from the place across from us. That plan didn't work out at all like I thought it would. Oh, I got the breakfast according to the plan. I climbed through the fence and went in the barn real silent as not to wake Gem.

Only she was awake and the special deputy from Lawrence had his pistol trained on her again. I held a plate of bacon and eggs with some hash browns in my left hand. I pulled my pistol with my right and real softly said, "Drop your pistol and get on your knees."

He replied much louder. "No and if you don't toss yours over against the wall, I will dispatch this little girly of yours to the Pearly Gates."

I shot him where he stood. I just didn't think this was the time for a debate.

"Mister this is the second time you pointed a pistol at her. You seem a slow learner."

He didn't answer.

I still had Gems breakfast in my hand, so I offered it to her. I didn't get the impression she was very hungry.

Murphy came through the front part of the barn, at the sound of the pistol report. He sized things up quick and said. "Get mounted and get gone. Go south and turn west at the cross roads. One of my men will bring the rest of your horses and gear."

"How will he find us?"

"He will."

"How will we know him?"

"You'll know him, of that have no doubt. Now go, I'll finish up here."

We lit out of there like the hounds of Hell were nipping at our heels. They were. Gem didn't get breakfast. We rode hard until dark. We stopped at a farm off the road and the woman fed us. I don't know if it was an act of kindness or the poor gal was starved for the spoken word.

She made full use of our time together demonstrating the English vocabulary and all its nuances.

We could either stay there and not sleep listening to her or get back on our horses and not sleep.

We rode on. We stuck to the road for two days. Mostly we saw freighters and wagons but there were other people as well. No one we met coming towards us showed much interest. One old farmer we passed sold us some squash and two frying chickens. Later that afternoon we came on a thick patch of trees and made camp. I say we made camp, it wasn't much. We had left everything we had at Murphy's barn.

It didn't matter much, we still got one of the chickens cooked and some of the squash. Gem stopped eating, she had a little drop of chicken grease on her chin. "That was an act of pure chivalry back there."

"I don't know about that."

"King Arthur and Maid Marion."

"I think it was King Arthur and Guinevere."

"The names matter not at all, you know what I mean. I'm telling you it was a brave and heroic act, you dolt." She leaned over and kissed me right on the mouth. My first thought was she tasted like chicken, my next thought was I didn't know what to think. My mouth went dry and my heart started pounding. This was new territory, I had no idea what it was, but I knew I liked it.

At first, I couldn't talk and when I could I said something about I didn't think it all that heroic. By killin that man all I did was set us farther down the outlaw trail. Before they didn't really know who, we were, now it would be common knowledge.

Gem took my hand and smiled. "You didn't kill him, he was alive when we left."

I knew no one could find us hidden in these trees and after a while I fell into a deep sleep. The next morning I awoke to a man standing over me saying something. "Tell the girl to come out from behind the tree, Murphy sent me to find you two. The man had on a broad brimmed black hat with a single long black braid of hair hanging down to almost the middle of his back. He had dark eyes and a dark beard with traces of white in it. The uniform jacket he was wearing proclaimed him to be a sergeant in the rebel cavalry.

As he was standing there talking I realized one of his legs was cut off at the knee and he had what I made out to be a two by four strapped to the outside of his thigh with two leather belts. One buckle said CSA, the other buckle said USA. Below the belts, where the stub of his leg rested, was an old horseshoe that had been heated and bent to form a small platform. About an inch up on the back side of his 'leg' was a horse shoe nail driven in, leaving the head of it with a little less than a quarter inch sticking out.

It didn't look like there was one single way to use that lash up that didn't hurt. All I could do was stare at him, finally I pointed at it and said. "What's the nail for?" It came out like I was simple minded.

"Good way to start the conversation, senor. I use it for a spur, someday I'm going to have a silversmith fit me with a fine silver rowel.

Gem came out from behind the tree still holding her pistol, although it was down at her side.

"If I may, my name is Sergeant Ernesto Benavides, cousin to Refugio, Christobal, and Colonel Santos Benavides commander of the 33rd Texas Cavalry and highest ranking Tejano in the Confederate Army.

Gem was staring at his leg or lack of it. "You speak pretty good American for being a Mexican."

"Little senorita, I was born, raised and educated in Texas. I went to college in Virginia for three years studying the fine art of engineering, before the war put an end to all that. We speak to each other same as you."

"I meant no offense."

"I took none. Murphy calls me Ernie, if you like, you can too."

"What's a Tejano?"

"If we live long enough, I will explain it to you. Right now, I suggest we shake and rattle on out of here. Pretty much this whole part of the world is looking for you two".

Gem got to callin him Sergeant Ernie and after a while so did I. Regardless of what we called him the man was a wonder. He did of course walk pretty funny. I should be clearer on this nobody, but nobody made fun of his impediment, except Sergeant Ernie himself. He could sit a horse as good as any man, I ever saw, including my British

GEM

Army trained father. The times we were skulking around in the woods hiding from this posse or that troop of federals he moved around as quiet as a cat.

One night it was pouring rain and we were holed up under a rock outcropping trying, to no avail, to keep dry. Gem asked him if the war had cost him his leg.

He looked right at Gem with those dark black eyes of his. Just as a bolt of lightning lit up the night sky and Sergeant Ernesto Benavides with rain dripping off the brim of his hat. For that instant in time he looked otherworldly, maybe even something out of the Old Testament. Then he said. "No, my mother did it."

"God in heaven, your own mother. What did you do to deserve such a fate?" Gem and I fancied ourselves battle hardened border ruffians who had seen most of it, but a mother doing this to her child?

He started laughing until the tears coming from his eyes were mixed with the rain. We had to wait for him to catch his breath. "By actual count I have said the same thing ten million times, and no one ever asked that question". He was still struggling to contain his laughter. "I heard once, it is said little red-headed girls that wear hats to cover their wild hair are blessed with special gifts the rest of us don't have." He stared into Gems eyes and Gem shivered but looked right back. The rain might have let up or maybe it didn't, it did not matter. He clearly had our undivided attention.

"Our family had at that time land grant ranches down on the South Llano River. We had lived there for generations. Raising cattle and fighting Indians was mostly what we did. Apaches usually but every now and again the Comanche would raid our part of the country. This fight was with them and it was bad, so they tell me. I was just a little Niño then and don't remember that one. My Grandfather, my father, my uncles, the women and the vaqueros that worked the ranch fought them to a standstill. My Grandfather sensed a weakness and mounted up every able-bodied man and attacked from the hacienda. It was a running battle for a week and when it was over that particular band of Comanche never ventured our way again."

We were still staring at him. "Right after the men left my mother discovered that somehow I had managed to get an arrow in my foot. The arrow didn't go all the way through my foot, it was just stuck there. She didn't think much of it and pulled it out. That should have been it, but as lady luck would have it that was not the case. My foot became inflamed and started swelling. My mother tried every trick she or the other women knew, nothing worked, and my demise seemed at hand. All the women consoled my mother and one of them gave her some fine linen to bury me in. The women left the room and found the priest.

Then prepared for the thing's women prepare for in times like that. My mother walked out from that room and said softly. "No by God, my son will not die." She made the sign of the cross and went to the kitchen and found a meat saw.

Gem and I looked at each other, what was there to say?

"I grew up without a foot, never knew what it would be like to have one. This may seem a little odd, but in the winter the toes I don't have get cold."

It just kept raining and raining. We were wet and cold for the next three days. We were all three just miserable. All we wanted was to be dry and out of the God damned rain. At one point we were hiding in the trees watching a Union patrol ride by.

Sergeant Ernie leaned over and whispered, "If this rain doesn't ease up soon my leg is going to warp."

After we got moving again Gem asked me if I thought the sergeant was joking around about his leg warping.

I said I thought yes, but that I really couldn't say. We could ask him. We decided not to.

It quit raining later that afternoon and we traveled hard for two more days. We covered a lot of ground, some of it was rough some of it wasn't too bad. It wasn't an easy ride but at least we were dry.

Sergeant Ernie knew a good place to camp in some scrub above the main road. He made a hell of a shot on a little buck, from the back of his horse. That deer had no idea we were even in the world.

The three of us lazed around and ate like kings. There was plenty of grass and the horses also lazed around and ate like kings. All of us needed the rest. The rain had been just as hard on the horses as it was on us.

Chapter XX

One day late in the morning Sergeant Ernie looked up from the little campfire we had and said. "Saddle up kids, they are almost here."

Gem jumped up. "Who is here? How do you know? Do we run, do we fight? Be clear Davey and I will not surrender."

Sergeant Ernie laughed and pointed at a dust cloud about two or three miles down the road. "That is Murphy and his caravan. My dear little 'soldado' I will miss you."

"What do you mean miss you?"

"You two are leaving the war, I am going back to it."

"Back, you don't have to go back. Come with us to Texas."

"I thought it was the Pacific Ocean you were bound for?"

How'd he know about our plan for the ocean? "Well, that is the plan."

"Could be after the war is over, I'll come out there and look you up?"

Gem teared up, I said. "Come with us, they got plenty of soldiers."

"There is not one thing in this world that I would rather do, but I told them I'd be back and that's what I'll do."

Mr. Richards grabbed me by the wrist. "People with true honor are rare but when you find them you will see they come in all shapes and sizes even a runty little Mexican with a two by four for a leg."

By around one o'clock we met up with each other on the road said hello to Murphy and goodbye to Sergeant Ernie. We hadn't known him long, still it was hard to see him go.

Gem asked me. "Is it the war or is it life in general that puts people into it, only to take them away?"

"Hell, Gem I was about to ask you the same question. I don't have the slightest idea how to answer it. I just know it is."

Murphy showed us our place in the line.

"First impression may seem to be disorder and to a certain degree that would be true, however there is a certain method to the madness and it gets better as it goes on."

I agreed to the first part. I was looking at what seemed a reenactment of Moses leading his flock out of Egypt. One of Murphy's men had been put in charge of our saddles and horses and I was pleased to discover my father's sword tied to one of the pack saddles. To be honest I had not given a lot of thought to it.

"You are not much of a shot, kid. That special deputy is, as far as I know, still among the living. I doubt we will see any more posse's hunting you two this far out. We will encounter Federal troops. They won't, I don't think, have much if any interest in you. Still when they show up make yourselves scarce."

While it was true that everyone was assigned to a certain spot in the overall order of the caravan. Very rarely did anyone really follow each other in line. A few times when Murphy thought there was a threat of Indian attack or other problem we lined out pretty well. Most of the time it was a spread out sort of affair. Just how spread out depended on the country and terrain. I don't know if one way or the other is better or safer, spread out meant a lot less dust to inhale. Lined out the wagon train used up close to a mile.

Gem and I were in the middle toward the back with the freighters and the Murphy personnel.

The wagon nearest to us was a Jewish family with a boy about ten and a colicky infant girl. Levi and Sally Hamovitz. He was a silversmith and engraver and a nice man. Sally was a big woman and her husband, with great

affection, called her round Sally. They had two
slaves they had bought to help on the trip.

"Whoa, Mr. Richards you are telling me a Jewish
family had slaves."

"Yes, it did seem odd to me at the time, but it was
still the law of the land. Lincoln had freed the slaves by
then. The Confederacy hadn't. The two slaves may have
been a couple or a brother and sister or total strangers for
all I know. I do know round Sally and the woman, I
cannot recall her name anymore, were best of friends."
Behind the Hamovitz were two wagons filled to
overflowing with Mormon pilgrims and their kids.
Behind them were four Quaker wagons and behind them
were the independent freighters and people walking or
riding a horse, bringing up the rear was a half dozen well-
armed men. Murphy's men.

"Mr. Richards excuse me for interrupting, that
seem a volatile group."

"It was Benny, it was. During the day everyone
got along well, simply because they had to. When we
were moving it was important to help each other. I will
say the conversations in the evening got lively."

"I'll bet."

"Nobody shot anybody, I did see a few fist fights
though."

"It's not hard to imagine, what did you do?"

"It was all about pick a side politics and Gem and
I stayed out of all of it. We did of course have opinions,
then again Gem and I were more or less on the dodge
from the law and didn't care to draw too much attention

to ourselves. I guess it is safe to say politics is still the same, only we seem more civilized now. We don't kill as many as we used to."

One morning word spread up and down the line Sally Hamovitz's baby had given up its ghost and died sometime in the night. Murphy stopped everything so the Hamovitz's could bury their child. Being they were Jewish, no one but their two slaves and Gem and I helped them put the baby in the ground. When we finished Murphy showed up and took off his hat and said it was time to go.

Mr. Hamovitz climbed up on his wagon and held down his hand to help his wife get on.

"Levi you go on, I will catch up." The dust rose as everything started to move. Out of that dust every woman on that train came and stood by the grieving mother. Nobody said a word and in unison all those women walked backward looking at the baby's grave until it was well out of sight before getting back on their various wagons.

Every preacher in every religion in the world will tell you God works in mysterious ways, they are right.

When we first started Gem would lead five mules and I led five. Gem and I tied our mules head to tail and kept them lined out behind us. Most of the others would pack their mules and turn them loose and herd them from behind, that system works fine.

Gem and I were too chicken to do it that way, those were Murphy's mules and we were not going to lose them. After a short time, the ten mules and the two mule skinners kind of started to learn what we were doing. One day I would lead all ten mules and the next day Gem would lead ten. On my days Gem would visit with Mrs. Hamovitz or some of the other woman. All of them liked her and all of them did their best to enlighten her to their way of thinkin.

Sometimes in the evening we might talk about the Mormon view or the Jewish one. We both had a hard time with the Quakers because all they ever talked about was living in peace and harmony.

Gem and I had been witness and lived through the Quaker sponsored Red Legs version of peace and harmony. I would go out with Murphy's hunters and help supply the caravan with fresh game. In the evenings when we camped, Gem would talk about God and the wages of sin and I would tell her about blowin up a young buck or a flock of turkeys.

One day Gem said. "You think I could go out with the hunters and you could talk hell fire and brimstone with those women?"

"I will not discuss theology with those women or any others for that matter."

"That seems one sided." Gem laughed and added. "I'm with you, I'm going to see Murphy about going out with the hunters."

"I suspect Murphy may seem one sided about that."

He wasn't at all, he told his hunters Gem would be going out with them and to see to it she returned, unharmed.

At first, they were reluctant, Gem wasn't much of a shot, but she was not at all bashful about jumping in with the cleaning and butchering and soon earned the respect of all of them. Although they never said anything, I got the feeling the hunters would rather go out with Gem. It took us a little over a month to get through the Indian Nation and into Texas. Things changed a lot In Texas. The wagons stayed closer together, the guard was doubled on the livestock, and everybody I mean everybody checked and double checked their weapons.

This was where the Comanche lived, this was their country and had been for a long time.

The settlers had pushed them back a little. When the war started most of the men left to fight and the Comanche's saw their chance to push back.

Murphy took me and Gem aside one day and expressed his feelings about Gem and I going out with the hunters. It struck me as a reasonable point of view.

"Bullshit!" Apparently Gem had a different take on it.

"What do you mean Bullshit little lady?" Murphy was not at all used to being second guessed.

"Just that, no one is going to tell me what I can or can't do. Even you Murphy!"

"Little lady."

"Don't you little lady me Mr. Murphy! Those hunters have come to depend on me and I will not let them down!" She turned and walked away.

Murphy and I looked at each other. "I guess she wants to go out with the hunters?"

"I guess she made her case clearly."

"What are you going to do?"

"What do you think I'm going to do?" Murphy looked at me and rubbed his chin. "I'm going to let her go. I hope to God I am not sorry."

When the Comanche's mounted their attack on the caravan it was random chance, just a roll of the dice that it happened when Gem and I were not out with the hunters. I wish we had been.

Gem and I had lived pretty much all our lives with war and violent death all around us. This was different, those Indians played in a different league with, if it's possible, a different set of rules and it was terrifying. The only warning we got was when the attack started. They came at us from both sides, howling and screaming. They came on fast, blink of an eye fast. Three of them rode right into the line in front of the Hamovitz wagon and behind me and Gem and our string of mules.

They killed Mrs. Hamovitz and her boy so quick we didn't even see it. Mr. Hamovitz could do nothing but sit there and watch, as the rest of his family was erased from his life. No sooner than they had rode through us, the three turned their horses around and came charging back. One of them jumped from his horse, pulled his knife and ran at me and Gem's mules.

I don't think the mules were what he had in mind, I think he wanted Gems red hair to hang in his lodge. The other two pulled up their horses and commenced to fire on us and Mr. Hamovitz. I became aware of more shooting off to my left and slightly behind me, it was Gem. She took the one on the ground out of the fight, before he even got very close to us.

It was a good shot. The other two Indians backed off.

Mr. Richards smiled at that memory.

While Gem and I and what was left of the Hamovitz family were living our part of the drama, the same thing was going on all up and down the line. It was fierce, it was horrible.

The screams from the Comanche attackers were enough, by themselves, to make your blood run cold. Add to that the noise of the wounded and scared horses and sounds of the gun fire were everywhere. Over and above it all, I could hear poor Mr. Hamovitz calling out for Round Sally. Again, and again.

Oh, my Sally, Sally, Round Sally what have they done to you. I don't remember if he called out for the boy or not. Just Round Sally.

Gem and I were still on horseback, holding on to Murphy's mules.

Gem came close and asked if I thought it might be a good idea to get off and fight from the ground?

That thought had not entered my mind at all.

"Yes, that might be prudent."

Before we did anything, one of the Indians very slowly and calmly walked his horse toward us and briefly looked down at the one Gem had killed. Then he looked hard at Gem, like it was important to him to remember her face. Then just as calmly and slowly as he had ridden up to us, he turned his horse around and rode off.

Gem and I both fired off a couple of shots at him, but we missed. That Indian did not even dignify our efforts by turning his head around to look at us, he simply rode away. The rest of them rode away too, hoopin and hollerin something awful. It was over. I don't know if it lasted ten minutes, if that long.

"Gem that Indian was riding my father's horse."

"Lord Nelson?"

"Yes, yes I think it was."

"Well, Davey I guess you would know."

I could tell she was doubtful, actually to tell the truth, I was too. It was pretty much of a stretch to think that Indian had Lord Nelson. Murphy had told me Goodnight was looking after him, for me.

The fight was over as quick as it started, but the rest wasn't. Besides the two Hamovitzs killed, there were three Mormons, one of them was another child. A little girl, I think. One Quaker woman and one of Murphy's freighters. Three or four others were wounded but not too seriously.

The Indians got away with four or five mules and ten horses. Three of them being two of the horses we got the day Felicity Brown was killed and the black with the two white socks we liberated from the special deputy.

Only one Indian was downed, that being the one Gem got.

Mr. Richards didn't make a sound for the longest time, then said to me, "Even on the ground dead, he was the God Damned scariest lookin human being I ever saw."

At this burial religion was everything and religion was nothing. Just about everybody had a horse in this race. The thoughts of the way of worship at that moment didn't mean much. Unless maybe for the dead Indian.

Two or three men drug him down off the trail and left him there for the coyotes. At the time I didn't think one way or the other about it. Now maybe I do. If Jesus Christ himself had shown up, you couldn't have found better fellowship. It lasted almost through the next day, when one of the Mormons and one of Murphy's teamsters started pounding on each other for some reason and things went back to normal.

Murphy rode up to us when he found out about Gem being the only one 'getting the job done' as he put it.

Gem asked him to please not tell the rest of the people.

He said that was all right with him, but why?

Gem told him she was more proud of hanging on to his mules during all the noise and confusion of the attack, than gunning down some godless savage.

Murphy smiled and gave her a kind of salute.

"I knew what Gem was thinkin and Benny, if you have been paying attention, so do you."

"You two were on the dodge."

"We were on the dodge." Mr. Richards laughed and those old eyes of his just sparkled.

"Would you mind driving me in to town in the morning?"

"Not at all."

"Good, thank you."

Chapter XXI

M r. Richards seemed to be on the road to recovery. He still needed the crutches and maybe he always would. I was happy he was coming around and more than happy to drive him to town. Our first stop was the feed store. I had to give Mr. Richards some help getting out of the pickup, although quite a bit less than I had in the past. The old guy just never ceased to amaze me. Maybe our future would include going horse back riding together again. As Mr. Richards was crutching his way into the office of the feed store a highly polished Ford five window coupe drove in the yard and Jeanie hopped out.

"Yo, rich boy! Come over here; there is someone I want you to meet." That model Ford had running boards and doors that opened from the front to the back, commonly known as suicide doors. Out of the driver's side door and on to the running board stepped a guy about my age, maybe a little older. He was tall, blond haired and was wearing a varsity letter sweater, from Lassen Union High School. I hated him.

Jeanie slipped her arm through his and said, with a big toothy kind of smile. "Benny this is Donald, Donald this is Benny. We shook hands.

I was at a loss for words, so I said. "Nice lookin Ford."

"Well." He replied, "My father owns the bank in Susanville. You wouldn't expect me to drive some old piece of shit, would you?"

Now not only did I hate him, I wanted to bloody his nose and mess up that perfectly combed blond hair. What was wrong with me? I didn't even know the guy. "No, no I guess I wouldn't." More important, what was wrong with Jeanie acting all moony eyed at this dickhead?

Mr. Richards came out of the office, looked over at us standing there and asked me if I was ready to go. Hell yes, I was ready to go! From however long it was from the office to the pickup, Mr. Richards had sized up what was going on in the parking lot. "She don't want no cowboy, Benny. That girl has set her sights set on bigger game."

"You want to go back to the ranch?" I was kinda short with my answer. God damn, I don't know why I was feeling like this. I really didn't even know her all that well. But God damn it! I felt like the wind had been knocked out of me.

"Not yet, I want to show you where I'm going to die. It's just up the street."

I forgot all about Jeanie and swiveled my head over at him. "Die?"

"Well, not today. I hope." He wanted to show me where he was going to live after my Dad took over the ranch. It was a tiny little house with a white picket fence around the front yard that was equally as small. He must have seen the sad look on my face. To my way of thinking a little house in town is not where any cowboy wants to end up.

"Benny don't look so sad, this is exactly where I want the finish line to be. There is a small barn out back and an irrigated pasture. I can keep a horse or two, if I want. I could not have picked a better place to cash in my chips. I just wish I could have Gem sittin on that little porch with me."

He sat in the truck, then, with his eyes looking straight ahead, somewhere. He didn't say a word and I could see the tears coming down his cheeks. "Enough of this old man shit. Help me out of this truck, Benny. Let's go look my new camp over." The tour was brief.

On the way back to the ranch Mr. Richards was full of life and telling me jokes and things of interest around Modoc County. "Benny if you will give me forty dollars a head for my little bunch of horses, I will give you Jake free of charge."

"Make it 35.00 and we got a deal." Oh man, that just popped out.

"I can see you are your father's son, make it 38 dollars and we have a deal." He held out his hand for me to shake on it.

Maybe I could have pressed it a little harder and got a better deal, it didn't seem right. We shook hands.

Mr. Richards asked me to drop him at the barn, when we got back.

I went up to the house and called my dad, to tell him my deal for the horses. I was second guessing myself about as fast as I could. What would Dad say? Would he be mad, would he be proud, most of all did I embarrass myself and would I have to go piss backwards and tell Mr. Richards we didn't have a deal after all?

"How do you think you did?" My Dad was calm when I told him how much of his money I had committed.

"I don't know, Dad, I may have paid more than I should have, maybe not."

"You say you got that Jake horse thrown in to boot?"

"Yes sir, Mr. Richards was clear on that."

"Only time will tell how good the deal was. If you like it and think it's a good one probably it's alright. Tell Mr. Richards when I come next week to take you back home for school, I'll bring the check."

I should remember the date of that day. My summer was about to end, I got all twisted up over a girl, I made my first horse deal (that I think passed muster with my father) and I knew I loved that old man, don't ask me to explain that, I just knew I did. I also knew after I left the ranch to go back to school, the chances of me ever seeing him again were slim to none. After breakfast I loaded some boxes Maggie had packed in the pickup.

Mr. Richards sort of waved his arm over the pickup bed. "Not much to show for all the years I put in on this planet."

"Sir, you have way more than a pickup load." That bothered me, maybe he was going to the new place with his death in mind.

"Oh, I know I do, it was just a figure of speech. I've got a lot. Don't be so God Damned serious about things."

I didn't think I was. It didn't take long to off load Mr. Richards's things. We went around to the back, so he could show me the pasture and barn. I thought it more of a three sided shelter than a barn. On the sunny side were two old wood chairs and a rickety lookin table.

Mr. Richards asked me if I might sit with him for a minute.

"Sure."

He made a comment or two about the pasture and barn and then sat a minute and started back in.

The first little settlement we came to after the death of his wife and son Mr. Hamovitz asked me and Gem if we could buy his wagon and team. Also, he inquired if we might have any interest in his two slaves, they were good workers. He had only bought them to help round Sally on the trip. "This is as close as I am ever going to be to my family, ever again. So, this is where I'll stay."

We bought his wagon and mules but said no to the purchase of his slaves. We didn't even have to talk about that part of it.

Gem asked him if he thought he would be alright here in this strange place.

"No, I don't believe I will."

The wagon train pulled out the next morning. Mr. Hamovitz and his slaves were nowhere to be seen. That more or less became the pattern from then on. Some people would leave the train. Murphy would sell some things from his wagons. Unload someone else's freight, load some more and move west.

Somewhere along in there, another trader bought all of Murphy's Dutch ovens. That put Gem and me out of a job. Murphy payed us off, right there on the spot, for hauling the ovens. He told us, if we wanted, he would trade us four of the best mules, we had been packing, for Mr. Hamovitz's four mules. If we would agree to stay with him as far as his ranch, he would consign us a load of freight and pay us accordingly when we got there.

"Will your ranch get us closer to the Pacific Ocean?"

"Yes Gem, I believe that case could be made."

That is how Gem and I got into the freighting business and it was good to us, off and on, over the years. Cows, I guess, treated us better in the long run. We worked our way across Texas for five more weeks. Murphy would unload and load. The number of people in the caravan dwindled the farther west we went. By the time we got to Murphy's ranch all that was left were me and Gem, Murphy, and five of his freighters.

It was a pretty spot on the Canadian River, not far from the New Mexico line. The house and outbuildings weren't much to look at, true, but overall it wasn't too bad a place. We pulled in the yard and a woman came out of the house with a little tow headed girl by her side. Murphy bailed off his horse and ran over to them.

Gem and I didn't know what exactly we should do, so we sat on the wagon and waited until the reunion was through. Murphy seemed embarrassed a little when he became aware of us looking at him. They started toward us and Gem and I climbed off the wagon to greet them. She was tall and lean and beginning to show signs of getting bleached out from the sun, I thought she was really pretty. I got the impression, just from lookin at her, she didn't suffer fools.

Gem kind of jabbed me in the side and said, "I think I like her, she wears men's trousers."

"And spurs." I added.

"Gem, Davey, I want you to meet my wife Lillie and our daughter Sadie. You two knew her mother.

"Knew her mother?" Gem asked and then said in a real small voice. "Felicity Brown?"

"Yes, Felicity Brown is my mother."

Murphy got a funny look on his face, it was easy to see he didn't want to say what he was about to say. "Was, these two were there when it happened."

Mrs. Murphy looked at Murphy and started to cry, Murphy looked at his wife and started to cry.

Gem started in, so did I. I don't know maybe the God Damned freighters were cryin too.

Mrs. Murphy stopped crying, straightened up and said. "Murphy unload those wagons and see to the livestock. You two come with me."

The house wasn't much to look at inside either, although it was neat and looked well organized. The cook stove had a nickel plated chimney and trim. I guess Mrs. Murphy had her cry and it was down to business.

"Tell me about my mother."

Gem and I looked at each other, not sure where to start.

"I know she traveled with whores and was one herself that does not mean I didn't love her and would want to know of the circumstances of her death." A tear came down her cheek. "Even though what you are about to tell me is no doubt grim, maybe worse."

"Gem can tell you more about how she died than I can. I'm going out and help Murphy with the wagons and stock."

Gem and Mrs. Murphy stayed in the house for a couple of hours. When they came out they both looked pale and had red rimmed eyes from crying. There is not the slightest doubt in my mind I chicken shitted the deal by leaving Gem alone to tell the circumstances of how and why Felicity Brown went to her final reward. I wasn't sorry.

That evening Gem told me some of their conversation and that Mrs. Murphy told her Murphy was going back to the war in a few days.

"Davey, she asked me if we might see our way clear to stay here for the duration of the conflict. She told me she could really use the help on the ranch with her horses. Davey, I said we would."

"You did."

"I did."

"Is this something we should talk over?"

"Talk all you want Davey, this is where we are staying, at least for the foreseeable future."

We stayed. We stayed until the south surrendered and the war came to an end. We didn't know it was over for a month or so.

Murphy came home with his wagons empty. For a while he didn't do much of anything but stare out at the landscape.

That didn't stop the rest of us. While Murphy was gone, Lillie Murphy had not been idle. She had built up a horse herd anyone would be proud of.

Gem and I were her colt starters, not horse breakers. "I want the horses I sell broke, not broken she would often say".

No one ever laid a hand or whip on one of Lillie Murphy's horses. Gem was a natural with a horse, I got alright at it, but I never was as good as Gem. I would try to take the rough off and Gem would put the polish on.

Shortly after we first got there, right after Murphy had gone back to the war. Gem and I decided we should give Felicity Brown's sack of money to her daughter and granddaughter. We both felt it was rightly theirs, not ours. Lillie hugged us, laughed and cried at the same time and said, "I'm going to ruin the day for a certain black hearted banker in town. He has had his eyes on this property for a while now. It's not enough to pay off the note, never the less we can buy ourselves some time."

Gem told her we had offered it to Murphy and he turned it down.

"He told me you did when he gave me the letter from General Lee."

"Why would he turn us down?"

"Pride is a funny thing in a man."

"If you knew about it, you could have just asked. It is your money, there is not one doubt about that."

"Pride is a funny thing in a woman".

After the war ended everything in Texas simply went to hell. Confederate money was no good, Yankee money wasn't much around. In Texas, at that time, a census taker would be hard pressed to find ten thousand citizens.

There was not much law, jobs were scarce. Cotton farming was no longer. Lillie Murphy's horse buyers no longer had money.

The banker that held the mortgage on the Murphy ranch went bust and disappeared with whatever money was left. Lillie had no idea if that put the ownership of the ranch in jeopardy. It was bleak times and the mood around the Murphy place clearly reflected it.

The Murphy's fought with each other on staying or going. Murphy thought the future for his family was back in Virginia and was all for leaving as soon as possible.

Lillie Murphy's view of the future was right there in Texas.

Gem and I tried to be as scarce as we could. You might be surprised how small a place can be, surrounded by thousands of acres.

One bright clear morning I was putting a ride on a nice bay colt when off in the distance I could see the dust made by several horseman. I knew it wasn't made by Indians, they were real good at not letting you know if they had decided to pay a visit. It was Sergeant Ernie with a group of men that looked a lot like the bushwhackers from Missouri. They were Texas Rangers in pursuit of Comanche's.

Gem hugged him, I shook his hand.

He must have done alright after the war, he had a new two by four. The army buckles were gone, replaced by finely engraved silver ones. The former Confederate army sergeant turned Texas Ranger had also mounted on it some silver and turquoise jewelry. To the delight of me and Gem and I'm sure more so to Sergeant Ernie there was a silver spur sticking out on the bottom with a rowel easily twice the size of a fifty dollar gold piece. It made us smile.

He told us the main reason he and the men came by was to ask Murphy if he would be captain and leader of this troop.

I got the feeling if it were not for his wife and child, he would have saddled his horse immediately. The Murphy's went in the house.

I knew he'd go with them, Gem felt the opposite and said, "There is no way Murphy will leave his family."

The next morning, he saddled up and left with the rangers.

Gem was disappointed and mad. "Why did he leave you, like that?"

Lillie Murphy held Gem in her arms for a moment, they both cried. "Gem, a man like Murphy can't live on a ranch like this. His place is out there leading those men or others like them. If he don't get killed, he will come back and declare his undying love and affection for me and Sadie. Then he will be gone again. That's who he is and that is who I love."

She went back in the house, Gem and I headed off for the corrals. "Davey don't for one second get the idea that will ever be acceptable behavior with us. Are we clear?"

"Yes ma'am." All kinds of things happened that summer after Murphy left. The first was Charlie Goodnight and a few men came to the ranch. He too was looking for Murphy. He recognized me and Gem right away.

"God damn, I never thought I would see you two again. The Lawrence Assassins, don't that beat all?" Then he got serious. "Damn it Davey, I apologize. I lost your horse to Comanche's, along with about thirty others."

I didn't mention that I had kind of figured that out.

"Before we go much farther I should tell you there is a man with a useless left arm looking for you two. Tells everyone he is a special deputy with a commission from Kansas and that in the dark of night you shot him in the back, ruining his arm."

"He is right in one regard, I did shoot him from behind. I don't suppose he made mention of him getting ready to kill Gem, if she didn't hand over some money he thought she had. At that time, he didn't think we were special deputy work, he was purely a man of low character prepared to take the life of a child for money."

"Be that as it may, he is looking, and the reward is five hundred dollars a head."

Gem found some humor in that. "I think we were worth more during the war."

"The reason I was looking for Murphy, I am going to take as many cows as I can get up to Kansas."

"I remember you talking about driving cows to Kansas. That was a long time ago, I'm glad to see you are doing it."

"There is no money in Texas, we all know that. The damned Yankees up north can't print it fast enough. I will make you the same deal I wanted to make Murphy. I will pay you four dollars a head for every longhorn you can find and capture. I will start north for Kansas in the fall. It is only right I tell you, your four dollar cow will bring fifty dollars up there. If you want to go with me, we— "

"Gem and I will not be going to Kansas."

"Don't sugar coat it, boy tell me what you think." He was laughing.

We were all laughing, when it slowed Gem looked up. "Mr. Charlie Goodnight there is not enough tea in China or money in this world that will draw Davey or I back to that God forsaken part of the world. Is that enough sugar coat for you?"

"Yes ma'am!"

Goodnight got down to it then. "I will set up some holding pens for whatever cattle you bring in. My rep will put your brand on the right side and my brand on the left. I will pay five dollars for steers and four dollars for open cows or heifers. Bulls are worth three dollars to me. I don't want any cow calf pairs, you can keep them and build up your own bunch. I will settle up when I come through. Sound alright to you?"

We agreed it did and shook hands all around.

Benny, in Texas after the war, wild cattle were everywhere and free for the taking. When I tell you they were wild cattle, I mean to say they were wild. Think about how a fellow might round up and drive a herd of white tails to Kansas. Those cows would feed at night and hide out in the thick brush during the day. At first, we tried to ride into the brush and chase them out. That produced poor results and beat up the horses and us. Lillie Murphy knew a guy that knew a guy and surprised us one morning with a half a dozen dogs she bought. I don't have the slightest idea of their breeding, but they were cow gettin sons of bitches. The work was never easy, though with the dogs it got some easier. They were not pets, they were not particularly friendly dogs. They were hard to be around and if you didn't pay attention, they'd bite you as soon as they would a cow.

On the good side of it, we wanted cows, not pets. Those dogs did the work of twenty men and took more abuse than any man could or would. Gem and I went out almost every day, sometimes Lillie would go with us. That woman was a hand.

Murphy would come home every so often and help us for a little while. He wasn't much of a cow hand, but that man could build a fence.

Of course, in the beginning Gem and I were just as pathetic as cowboys as Murphy was. The difference being, we wanted to learn how to do the work and Murphy never showed much interest. It wasn't all that long before Gem started to think like a cow, it took me longer. That girl knew what a cow was going to do, before the cow knew what it was going to do. Goodnight was correct when he told us the cows were thick as fleas. After we started getting better at it, Gem and I started bringing in respectable numbers.

Chapter XXII

M r. Richards stopped talking and started having a coughing fit. When he was through coughing, he said. "He who teaches himself has a fool for a teacher." He laughed. "I believe it was a fellow named Shakespeare said that and he knew what he was talking about. If he hadn't been born a couple hundred years before we were, I would swear he had me and Gem in mind."

When the summer was over, and we tallied up with Goodnight, we had done alright. He asked us again if we cared to ride to Kansas and get the big paycheck.

"No!" We both said at the same time.

Lillie jumped in. "I too have no desire to see Kansas. However, if some of my horses made the trip?"

Goodnight held up his hands in mock self-defense. "How many and how much?"

Lillie and Goodnight made their deal and I think he went north with at least a few good horses.

Lillie, Gem and I split the money from the cows and horses and decided maybe this was not too bad a way to earn a living. And it was for a couple of years. We all made some money, built up the Murphy ranch, and supplied cattle to Goodnight and others making drives north.

Gem and I liked it there and probably would have stayed in Texas, except for this government program they liked to call reconstruction. The plan was to redistribute the land of the wealthy plantation owners and make sure the freed slaves got their piece of the pie. To carry out the plan first came Marshall Law with soldiers. Shortly thereafter came what was to become the infamous carpetbagger.

People were dying and gettin shot up on more or less the same scale as before the war.

The south had lost the war true enough, still old habits die hard. Texas and the rest of the south, for that matter, wasn't much interested in changing their ways.

We got caught up in it one beautiful fall day. We were preparing to take our last bunch of cattle to Goodnight's pen. A two horse open surrey carrying two men, followed by half a dozen mounted blue coated soldiers came in the yard. One of the men identified himself as the new sheriff for the county. The other one Lillie Murphy knew, it was the same banker that had snuck out of town with what was left of the depositor's money.

"Mrs. Murphy nice to see you again." His voice sounded, for lack of a better way to put it, like an outhouse smells. "After a close check of the banks records, this ranch is in default." When he smiled he looked the reason the outhouse smells.

The sheriff produced a piece of paper from his inside suit pocket. "You have two weeks to vacate the premises." He dropped the sheet of paper on the ground, tipped his hat, and they left.

If Murphy had been there the results of that day might have been different, but he wasn't. Gem spoke first, "to Hell with them!"

"What are we going to do?" I asked. Lillie bent over and picked up the paper. Read it, shook her head, wadded it up and threw it back to the ground. Gem and I stood there, stunned, I guess you could say. Lillie wasn't.

"Davey you and Gem finish rounding up the cows that go to Goodnight, take ours too. Capture all the horses and take everything to Goodnight's pens. I will meet you there later."

"What's that mean later?"

"What that means is I need everything gone." She smiled her sweet smile. "There is going to be a fire."

"A fire, you can't mean that, all the work and time you put in this place."

"That is exactly what I mean. That son of a bitch banker thinks he's the smartest guy in town, maybe he's not. There is no court for me to take this to, there's no one to buy it, and there is the cold hard fact of not much I can do."

"There has to be a better way."

"There is not. Another thing to give some thought to is, I live with the famous Lawrence Assassins and I don't want that puss gutted sheriff sniffin around you two."

"We can take care of ourselves, Lillie Murphy. You don't have to throw it all away to protect me and Davey, God Damn that banker to hell". Gem was fired up.

"Oh sweetie, we're not giving up anything. We still have some money, our cows' and horses. West of here is better and cheaper land. All that sold out banker is going to get from us is a pile of charcoal." She smiled and added. "I suspect Murphy and Mr. Banker will have a chat about all this."

It took Gem and me close to the two weeks to gather and drive everything south to Goodnights pens. Lillie Murphy arrived around the same as time Gem and I.

Murphy and some of the rangers came a few days later with Murphy's wagons and the one that belonged to me and Gem. Sergeant Ernie was driving our wagon. When he climbed down to give it to us, I could see he had added more turquoise and silver to his two by four.

"That leg of yours gettin kinda heavy?" Gem asked.

"You think it is too much, little senorita?"

"No, no on you it seems tasteful."

Murphy gathered us around, he was holding a flour sack. "Before I got here, I had a heart to heart with the new sheriff and the old banker. It is comforting to know, in these times of trial and tribulations, what can be achieved with pleasant conversation between responsible adults. The new sheriff decided that job opportunities in east Texas were far superior to those available in west Texas and got on his horse and left town, even before our pleasantries were over. The banker it turned out was a truly kind hearted soul after all. He offered to buy the Murphy Ranch at whatever I thought was a reasonable price." The flour sack was filled with Yankee greenbacks.

"He at some point in time may have a change of heart. In case of an outcome like that, what might your thoughts be on heading for the New Mexico line? In a hurry?"

We all left for New Mexico in the morning. Whether the banker changed his mind or not, we had no trouble along the way. At the border the rangers and Sergeant Ernie parted company with us and went back to being rangers in Texas. That was the last time we saw or heard from or about Sergeant Ernie. Over the years Gem and I would wonder what had happened to him. Gem always said she hoped he was able to add a lot more jewelry to his two by four.

New Mexico had different Indians and we got acquainted with some of them on a hot

afternoon not too far from Santa Fee. A couple of
days before we tangled with the Indians, we met
up with a troop of Union Calvary. I can't say how
long they had been out, I can say they looked
rough. Their horses and pack mules were used up,
the men were used up. They looked as ready to
fight a swarm of Indians as your grandma might.
The officer was a captain and the way he looked
and sounded, gave us the impression he was
barely hanging on to his men and his command.

"We are on our way back to the fort, we
have spent the last two weeks tracking Dapper
Charlie and his gang of cut throats."

"Dapper Charlie?"

"You never heard of Dapper Charlie?"
The way he said that, implied we must be a pack
of fools and highly irrational pilgrims, fresh from
a Sunday social. "Dapper Charlie is pure evil
dressed in a three piece wool suit. The word is he
was taken from his tribe and raised by a hard shell
Baptist family from Iowa. When he was about
fifteen or so he slit their throats and made his way
back to this part of the country robbing and killing
pretty much every step of the way.

"Whew, "Lillie looked at Murphy. "None
of this sounds like anything we might be
interested in."

The soldier spoke again. "No ma'am he is
not, although he speaks flawless English he has
never been known to make any bargains. He'd as
soon kill you and yours as speak." No one said

anything, everybody seemed bolted to the spot they were standing. "As the representative of the Grand Army of the Republic in this territory, I am ordering you to turn these wagons around and follow this troop back to our duty station."

Murphy looked up at the captain sittin on his wore out horse and maybe you could say it was a smile. "Captain, I believe in my heart of hearts you have only the best of intentions to the wellbeing of everyone in this little wagon train and I have nothing but respect for you for that."

The captain started to say something, Murphy held up his hand.

"Sir, again with all due respect I have never taken an order from a Yankee son of a bitch yet and I am more than positive I will not start now this late in the game, sir.

Gem and I, well everybody held their breath. How was this going to end? The captain looked at Murphy, twisted a little in his saddle and pointed.

"I'd say it is three or four days to Santa Fe in that direction, sir." He signaled to his men and they rode off.

Lillie spoke first, "Murphy what in the hell was that?"

"Aw, I don't know, Lillie. It was that Grand Army of the Republic horse shit, I guess." We moved out and everyone paid very close attention to their weapons.

We rolled along for a couple of days as peaceful as could be and kind of let down our guard. We had stopped for the day, by a small stream. We had no clue they were there and then they were all around us.

I guess I might use the word polite, to describe the way they wanted to rob us. It was plain to see Dapper Charlie was the man in charge. The Yankee was right in his description, the man was well-dressed in a suit and tie. What the Yankee Captain failed to mention was how tall Dapper Charlie was.

After it was all over, I figured out the soldier probably hadn't ever seen him. He was mounted on a beautiful big red roan, and he rode it right into our camp, bold as brass. He spoke better English than any one of us. "This is the deal I propose to you people. If I am allowed to take that girl with the red hair to be one of my wives, I will let some of you live to tell the story of how you escaped the wrath of Dapper Charlie. I will naturally take all the wagons and livestock"

"No!" Lillie stepped from behind the wagon with her twenty gauge bird gun and fired.

Dapper Dan sagged a little in his saddle but didn't fall from the horse. That was the cue every single person opened fire, us and them.

It got hot, bullets were flying everywhere, and I saw one Indian go down, although it wasn't me that got him. Dapper Charlie tried to ride around the wagon to get to Lillie, she ducked back under the wagon and when she came out the other side she fired again. Lillie didn't know how bad or if she had even hit him at all, but it took the fight out them.

Murphy looked around to see if any of us were hurt. "God damn, Lillie you shot Dapper Charlie and then you got his horse right square in the ass. I guess he and us will be telling the story with a different ending, then he had planned."

Lillie walked over to Gem and hugged her. They both started to cry. "No bastard, son of a whore outlaw is going to take this pretty little red headed girl for his wife as long as I am on this planet."

"No by God, I'd say he won't." Murphy went on. "In a way I feel sorry for poor old Dapper Charlie."

"How's that Murphy?" I asked.

"The poor heathen had no idea he was up against Felicity Browns daughter."

We made it to Santa Fe a few days later with no further adventures. The Marshall in town told us we were lucky to be alive, the general outcome of Dapper Charlie and his gang was death and bedlam.

Naturally, because he was the law, he wanted our thoughts on why Dapper Charlie did not get the upper hand and dispatch us on the spot. I got the feeling he thought we did something wrong, because we were not killed and scalped.

Despite the facts of bad outlaws and unfriendly law officers, Lillie Murphy immediately fell in love with Santa Fe. I didn't care one way or the other. Gem hated it.

The freight business in that part of the country and up towards Arizona was booming. Freighters and mule packers were in high demand. The Murphy's, Gem and I fit right in and started making money right away. We stayed through the winter.

Mr. Richards stopped talking, like he was struggling with something. "Benny, that was the winter Gem and I found out what it was like to be more than spies and Missouri border outlaws. We discovered what has been described as the pleasures of the flesh. I don't know how to talk about this."

"That's alright Mr. Richards, you don't need to." I was as embarrassed as he was. He gave me a big smile and slugged me on the arm.

"In those days my ol tally whacker would get so hard a cat couldn't scratch it and Gem and I took full advantage of it. You know Benny how it feels in the spring and the weather gets nice. Add all that into the mix and life is good, you feel good, real good."

"Yes sir, I will take your word for it."

Mr. Richards was tickled with himself and his memories. I wasn't so much. I guess he could see that because he stopped talking about the birds and bees and started back in.

Gem and I were harnessing the mules for a load we had going to a silver mine north of town. "Davey, I want to see the Pacific Ocean."

"I don't know Gem, we are doing pretty good here."

"We don't need to live in this rock pile to do good, Davey." Gem was right and if the truth were to be told, I was not opposed to her line of thinkin. I wanted to see the ocean too.

"Ok let's figure it out." The travel plan was not all that hard, there were groups of people moving all over the country. We put together a little bunch of longhorns and joined up with a company that had elected a man that referred to himself as Major Mark Shelley, to be the leader and we could call him Major Shelly. If this fellow had been a major, I can't imagine what army was dumb enough to put him in a leadership role.

He said his plan was to go straight west through Arizona and on to California and end up near the ocean south of a place called Los Angeles. He made it sound easy. That proved not to be the case. The hardest part was leaving the Murphy's. This may sound melodramatic I know that, but it was.

The Murphy family was the only family Gem and I had. They were stable and solid in a world that wasn't.

Lillie, more and harder than Murphy, fought tooth and nail for us to stay. Don't let me give you the impression Murphy didn't put up a battle, that wouldn't be right. He did. I think in his world it was expected behavior, but he loved his wife and championed her cause as best he could.

Every argument they presented for staying, and there were plenty, was right. When the day came to leave, we were so full of doubts we could have stayed. We didn't, we couldn't.

Although there were many times when we would question the wisdom of our decisions. Deep down inside, we both knew we were right. Santa Fe was the Murphy family future, not ours.

Gem and Lillie wrote letters back and forth until Lillie passed away, in the fall of ninety-one. We heard Murphy moved back to Virginia after she died, and we lost all contact. Gem got a letter once from Sadie telling us she had moved and married and had two children. She had named them David and Gemmy, but she left no return address.

The last thing Murphy said to me was, don't let Dapper Charlie eat you two. He didn't. Major Shelley had pretty much sugar coated his version of what all was entailed. Not only the actual journey but his ability to lead.

The trip was one miserable event after another. Most of the time the 'major' would ride out of camp for the day and return after we had stopped for the night. "I think we are doing right, I think we are heading in the right direction, be strong God is holding our hand."

There was little water or feed. Mules died, wagons broke down and had to be left behind.

Even our "famous for living on little or nothing" longhorns suffered, and we lost most of them. It became a one foot in front of the other slog, through a horrible browned out part of the country. No one died and one woman had a baby. I think it was a girl, I don't remember anymore.

Despite the lack of action or decisions from the 'major' we made it to the Pacific Ocean. They have not printed enough money, to ever get me to set foot in that part of the world again. Still, that first view of the ocean is something like no other.

"You ever see the ocean, Benny?"

"Yes, sir I have, and you are right it is truly a sight to behold."

"This chair beside the barn is going to be a nice place for an old man to be. Maybe I should finish off my run sitting here writing my memoirs? Think that's a good idea, Benny?"

"Yes, sir I do, maybe they will make a movie about you."

"Well, if they do, I want that tall guy Cooper to play me, the resemblance is plain as daylight."

"There is no denying you two could pass for twins, I'll bet he'd be tickled."

"I'm sure he would, probably do it for free."

On the way back to the ranch I asked. "How did you end up here, it's a long way from the ocean?"

Los Angeles wasn't much of a place then, most of the action was up the coast in San Francisco. The padres had come up from Mexico and settled most of the southern part of California with a series of missions scattered along the coast. Their main job was saving souls and one of the ways they did it was with work. The hide and tallow trade was the mainstay of the missions and provided jobs for the poor heathen Indians, while they were learning to be soldiers for Christ. At first the Indians were not allowed to ride horses and tend to the cows. It didn't take all that long for the herds to build up so big, the padres had to start teaching the Indians and low born Mexicans how to ride.

Up until then the riders were for the most part, classically trained Spanish noblemen and former soldiers. Out of this mix of horsemen and Indians there evolved a style of horsemen that few had ever seen. Not so much that they could ride their horses, everybody the world over could ride horses.

The weather was almost always pleasant, and the country was more or less wide open. Raising cattle under these circumstances was easy. Vaqueros as they became to be called, had all the time in the world to learn about the horse. Hell, Benny I know, you know all this. Gem and I didn't, and it captured us.

In Texas to gather cows it was hard work, in California it was fun. By the time Gem and I got there the mission system was long gone. The gold rush had changed all that and the vast open spaces were being settled. Different people were raising the cattle now and

Gem and I found work buying and selling cattle, right away.

"Benny will you park the truck over there?" Mr. Richards pointed toward the barn. "I don't feel the need to move anymore furniture today."

I parked and went around the truck to help Mr. Richards. At the same moment, in a big cloud of dust, Jeanie pulled up next to us. Mr. Richards looked at me and kind of gave me a little smile. "I'll go check with Maggie on the status of dinner."

I watched him slowly crutch his way toward the house.

"Where you been hiding, Benny? I haven't seen you in so long I was wondering where to send the flowers."

"I don't know that I have been hiding."

"Then where in the hell have you been?"

This girl was doing it to me again. "Donald?"

"Oh pashoo, Donald don't mean nothin."

"That is not the impression I got."

"Don't spend a lot of time worrying about impressions, I'm here now."

"Donald throw you in the outhouse, did he?"

"Benny how could you even think such a thing?"

I stood there and looked at her, truth is, I couldn't think of anything to say. Jeanie got a pouty sort of look on her face. Shit, this is one cute girl, I felt myself weaken.

"Her name is Susan and her dad owns the big sawmill, on the south end of town." Now it was a woe is me look.

"Aw Jeanie I feel bad for you, I do."

"You do? Will you stop by the feed store and visit me?"

"Sure." I watched her tail lights as she drove out of the yard. I knew I wouldn't make any big effort to see her again. Mr. Richards was right, she was too much girl for me. I walked up to the house and didn't feel at all bad.

Mr. Richards and I emptied out the tack room and his leather shop, loaded in the pickup and drove down to his new house.

The new place wasn't set up for any of it. We piled it up on the floor. Mr. Richards told me this was going to be his first project when he moved in.

We went back around back to the chairs and Mr. Richards began again. I got a feeling there might be a sense of urgency in his tone. I hoped we weren't getting close to the end, in more ways than one.

Even though the longhorns that survived the trip were in rough shape we were able to sell them right away and we started up the coast toward San Francisco. That became our life for a few years. We would find a spot with some grass and water. Sometimes we would find the owner and lease it. Most times we simply set up camp and ran the cows until we used up the grass or the owner ran us off.

We lived in the Hamovitz's wagon. Gem set it up on the inside in a very useable and homey way. A bushwhacker's idea of a home, anyway, I guess. Somewhere that summer we met up with an old man and a small boy, dressed similar in style to how Gem looked when we first met.

They were in a wagon loaded with various and sundry things he was trying to peddle or trade. Gem made a deal for some metal dishes and a coffee pot. You may recall the one we had, had a big dent in it. The boy said he would be proud to take the dented one in on the trade. Wedged in amongst everything else in the wagon was an old army surplus camp stove made of sheet metal.

I thought she paid too much money for it and I told her so.

Gem laughed at me and said. "Time will come when you will sing another song."

"I doubt that."

"I won't make you put your apologizes in writing."

We set it up near the back of the wagon where it was easy to move in and out. In warm weather we would take it out of the wagon and use it to cook on. Gem did a heck of a job on that wagon and it was comfortable and nice. Nowhere near as nice as Felicity Brown's wagon, but it worked great. Gem named it the Grand Hotel Hamovitz.

Mr. Richards stopped talking.

"You ok, sir?" He still didn't say anything. "Mr. Richards!"

Chapter XXIII

I t was like he had just shut down, I reached over and touched his shoulder. He jumped a little.

"Sorry Benny, those were some of the absolute best years Gem and I had. I'm not telling you the rest was bad, that would not be true or even close. Gem and I------." He stopped again and sat there.

I didn't say anything either. We, both of us sat there with the sun on our face, lookin out at nothing. Mr. Richards seemed to straighten a little and smiled. Like I said that was how we lived.

Buy some cows, sell some cows, and move on north. That part of the world does not get much in the way of winter and the living was easy. Somewhere south of San Francisco we had found what for all intents and purposes looked like a good place to spend the winter.

We rode into the little wide spot in the road that passed for the town, to inquire about the property. It wasn't really much more than a stage stop and a general store.

Nobody knew anything about anything beyond their lives at the stage stop. Gem and I were about to leave when the stage pulled in and unloaded its passengers. They were all well dressed, and they gawked at me and Gem as much as we gawked at them.

One of the passengers came over to where we were doing our gawking and introduced himself. "My name is Robert Cornmesser the third, of the south bay Cornmessers, do you two live and work around here?"

Gem gave her sweet smile. "No, sir just passing through."

When he smiled back at us I could see he had this little well-manicured mustache that seemed to be mounted perfectly on his upper lip. "Well, you never know when a fella might make a sale." And he handed Gem his business card.

R. Cornmesser III Limited

Purveyors of fine liqueurs and sprits

We both looked it over and to be polite, nodded our head in approval. "I don't have much interest in any of this." I pointed at his card. "I would like to buy that newspaper sticking out of your pocket, if you don't want too much."

"Ten Cents"

"Ten cents, crosses the too much line." Gem offered.

"You're good kid, let me know if you ever want a job in sales. He handed it to Gem, "Take it, it is a week old anyway.

"Thank you."

After he went in the stage stop building Gem turned to me.

"What are these things on the card?"

"Busthead in fancier bottles, I think."

"And to get a job in sales?"

"I think you have to grow a real tiny mustache on your upper lip."

We never got around to reading the newspaper until the next morning. "Gem, Gem come here and listen to this." I was reading the newspaper. "Noted cowman and blazer of trails from Texas to Kansas Charles Goodnight. Got caught up in a scrape with a bad Indian that goes by the name of Dapper Charlie and his band of renegades. The end result of this predicament was the death of Mr. Goodnight's dear friend and business partner, a Mr. Oliver Loving. A well-known and respected cattleman in his own right."

Mr. Goodnight is quoted as saying "I will not leave him buried in this God forsaken country." He commissioned the local blacksmith to build a coffin made of tin cans, flattened and soldered together. As of the time of this printing the departed man is being freighted back to southern Texas. When asked, Mr. Goodnight is quoted as saying: "I will not be accompanying my friend and partner back to Texas, we will meet up at his grave, when I return."

He is also quoted as follows: "I have a commitment to deliver these bovines and I mean to honor that." Mr. Goodnight continued. "I also have made a commitment to track down and have what I guess could be called a forty-four caliber conversation with one Mr. Dapper Charlie." And finally, he added: "God have mercy on his soul."

This reporter was not entirely clear on whether Mr. Goodnight was referring to his late departed friend or to the outlaw Dapper Charlie.

"Did that newspaper say anything about killing that Indian?"

"No, it didn't, I suspect it didn't get done, however I have a good idea it will. Goodnight is no slouch."

"Oh Davey, I remember that Indian. He scared me more than the Comanche that rode up and looked me over, after the attack on us back in Texas."

"That Comanche was far more of a fright to me than the all dressed up in a fancy suit, thief could ever be."

Gem hugged my neck, "Maybe we ought not dwell too much on scary Indians from our past."

She walked away, and I went back to the newspaper, but not for long. "Gem I guess I'm not done, in terms of dwelling on our past, that is. Wait till you hear what is on page three above the want ads."

"What are they talkin about now, I hope nobody has found Lord Nelson. That horse has caused us enough grief."

"No, no one that I know of has found him, yet. Although somewhat along the same lines, I think this article will be of interest to you. The Pinkerton Agency has come out with a list of the most wanted outlaws in America."

"Is Dapper Charlie's name on the list?"

"No, but mine is."

"What!"

"It is pretty low on the list, a ways below the James brothers and Cole Younger. You remember them?"

"I remember I lost the pistol, the one James brother gave you and I remember when we all met up by the side of the road, right after Felicity got killed. The name Younger I don't recall."

"He served with Quantrill and he was the one that rode up from the back of Felicity's wagon that day and handed us the wanted poster."

"Davey, I don't give two hoots about any of that, what about your name on this list?"

"Let me read it." 'Through sound and through investigation methods we at the Pinkertons have at long last ascertained the name and description of the leader of the notorious Lawrence Assassins. His name is David Richards formally of Kansas. He is described as being nearly six foot two inches tall and weighing around two hundred twenty pounds. He dresses in a sloppy manner and contrary to habits in attire he seems to prefer being clean shaven.'

"Six two in your dreams, Davey."

"Gem!"

"Sorry, continue." She smiled. "You would look good being that tall, you think it will happen?"

"Gem, mind if I continue?"

"Ooohoo Davey Richards six foot two."

"Gem, damn it, this is important!"

"Go on, Davey."

'There is no real description of the other assassin, other than the general look of a ferret on his face and around his eyes. Their trail of death and destruction tapered off in Georgia for a while then surfaced again in Texas. When they teamed with the James Younger gang to rob a banker of his honest profits. The Pinkerton Agency has named Tom Parsons, who proudly served with Jim Lanes Kansas Redlegs during the late war of the rebellion, as agent in charge.

Mr. Parsons, who was severally wounded in defense of his country, is quoted as saying despite his badly mangled arm nothing can or will stop him in his pursuit of justice. Could there be a finer example of a patriot? The Pinkerton Agency will appreciate any assistance given to Agent Parsons and have also offered a monetary reward for the capture and conviction of these two desperados. Extreme caution should be used when approaching, they are well armed and considered very dangerous.'

"Gem do you think we know this fine example of Kansas manhood?"

"Yes, I believe we do. Correct me if I'm wrong, this outstanding Union patriot tried to pay us back for saving his life by attempting to rob us not once but twice."

"I think you are right, I think it is him. If that turns out to be true, what are we going to do?"

"I don't know Davey, if it is him or not. It don't matter much, he will never find us in California."

"That's true we are a long way from Texas."

Gem started to laugh. "Agent Parsons and I have something in common."

"What's that?"

"We are both lookin for that six foot two fella."

Mr. Richards stopped talking again and stared off into space. This was getting harder and harder for him to do.

"Mr. Richards do you think we ought to be heading back to the ranch?"

"That's probably a good idea, Benny."

We got in the truck and drove back, Mr. Richards never said a word. I pulled up next to the house for him to get out, but he didn't.

"I'm startin to see the Angel of Death more and more in my mind, Benny."

"Oh no, sir please don't talk like that."

"Don't worry, I've been one step in front of that son of a bitch my whole life. Now come around and help me out of this truck and do not mention any of this bull shit of me seein death angels talk to Maggie, understand."

"Yes, sir I understand."

"Thank you, Ben, thank you for everything."

The way he said it was so final sounding, it scared me. He crutched to the house, just before he went in he turned around and looked at me. He didn't smile or wave, he simply looked at me for what seemed a long time before he turned and went in the house.

I went down to the barn and made some work for myself. I wanted no more of Mr. Richards's seeing angels and talk of his eminent demise. I thought work would keep me from thinking about it. It didn't.

Chapter XXIV

Maggie called out after a while and I went back up to the house for dinner. At dinner the talk turned to horses, Mr. Richards was full of life and told some more wonderful horse stories of good and bad horses.

I enjoyed the stories and tales; I did. Still I couldn't quite get the thoughts of death and angels far from my mind.

The next morning Maggie told me Mr. Richards was not feeling well and figured on staying around the house kind of resting up and for me to help her load up some more of, in his words, plunder.

We loaded more things in the truck and I made a trip to town and unloaded it. Mr. Richards's house was starting to look empty and this probably sounds dumb, lonely. For all those years it had been full of life and all that goes with it. Now it was beginning to look old and tired, used up. Now it was beginning to look like Mr. Richards.

Maggie and I loaded up again and I made ready for another trip to town. Truth be known, I was starting to not like the place much anymore.

I asked Maggie if she wanted to go with me and arrange the furniture.

"No." I had never seen such a sad expression on her. "You do it. I don't think it is going to matter much how it looks."

She scared me. "I think it will matter!"

She turned and walked in the other direction and left me standing there. Maggie Pete was beaten, her best was not going to be enough. Some things you can't fix. I wasn't as smart as Maggie, I thought it would mean something.

I set upon arranging the furniture and things in, to my mind, a way they both would like it and be able to use it. I won't tell you I chicken shitted in any way setting up the house, I maybe could have done a better job, I don't know.

I do know, and I will tell you with absolute certainty I poured my heart and soul into Mr. Richards's rawhide working shop. If I never accomplished anything for the rest of my life, that old man was going to finish out his days with a good place to work. He never saw it.

I got back to the ranch late, Maggie was waiting with a sandwich and some potato salad, she had been crying.

"He is back in bed on the back porch and don't want to get up anymore."

"What should we do?" The tears started to flow.

"In the morning you go make him get out of that bed and don't take no for an answer."

"Shit, Maggie I will try but I kinda doubt there would be a reason on this planet he would or should pay any attention to whatever I might say." The house was bare and seemed cold. Most of the furniture was gone, Maggie and I sat on a couple of old straight-backed wood chairs and looked at each other. All the pictures were gone, the radio was gone. Mr. Richards's father's sword was gone. All the life, all the things that brought joy and happiness were gone.

I couldn't help it, I began to cry and the more I looked at Maggie and the more I thought of Mr. Richards, the harder I cried. I have no idea how long we sat there crying.

Maggie made the first move when she got up and put my head to her chest and hugged me for all she was worth. It would be impossible to say whether it was the hug or having my head buried in that enormous bosom of hers, but I stopped crying and felt some better. "That is the end of all that, no more tears, tomorrow is a new day. Go upstairs and get some sleep. I'm goin out on the back porch and sit with Davey for a while, I'll see you in the morning."

Without belaboring the message of love for an old Indian woman; it's true I did. I tried to roust Mr. Richards from his bed the next morning; he was quite clear in his intention to stay right exactly where he was and no amount of whining from me was going to have any impact on his thought processes.

"Understand."

"Yes, sir I believe I do."

"Good now pull up that chair, sit down and shut up I want to finish my story once and for all." The way he said that last part I thought I might start to cry again; I didn't.

After the war and for maybe twenty years a big part of the country lived with violence and sudden death. The south had lost the war but nobody living in that part of the country was particularly sorry or repentant. People were dying with almost the same regularity as during the war. There was only one army involved, so the scale was less.

The government passed laws every other day meant to protect the former slaves and redistribute the land. These were called free labor policies. It didn't mean freed slaves worked for free. It meant they were free to work.

It don't take a genius sort of brain to see a whole bunch of people who had just fought and lost, in what they referred to as the 'war of northern aggression' would not take kindly to such radical sentiments. Men with hoods and masks were everywhere, it paid poorly to be out at night.

When people came on a covered bridge, if they were on horseback it would be in the best interest of the rider to dismount and walk through. That way it might be possible to avoid getting tangled up with the legs of the men and women that got hung from the rafters the night before.

If you happened to be in a wagon with a cover, the canvas might have a smear or more of blood or worse yet body parts.

In the north people were dying in labor riots and trying to form unions. Out in the west and southwest the government had an entirely different set of ideas for dealing with the Indians. No free labor policies for Indians. The powers to be in Washington wanted them dead or somehow out of the way.

There was no shortage of jobs if a fellow was inclined to be a soldier, you could almost pick where you wanted to kill people.

Mr. Richards paused then started again. "Did you know, Benny about the same time Custer was getting wiped out at little big horn, the people in New York were building the Brooklyn Bridge?"

"No sir I didn't."

"Well they were, and railroads were being built all over the place. So much modern progress was going on, yet people were still dying left and right, violently."

Mr. Richards paused again, I think he was pissed. He was silent for so long I thought we were through for the day and I started to get up to leave. Before I could get up, he reached over and grabbed my wrist, his hand had just about enough skin on it to keep it from qualifying as a skeleton. The strength I felt that first day when we shook hands was gone. "California, let me tell you about California, please."

"Sure, please do." It felt in that room at that moment, in the race to battle his angel maybe he had lost a step or two and the son of a bitch was closing in. I hoped not.

"People were subjected to violence in California too, just not as much it seemed." Mr. Richards gained a step in his race.

The weather was mild, the grass was always green. Gem and I had made it to the Pacific Ocean. Gem and I had truly escaped the war. Life was good, and Gem and I could see no clouds in our future.

In the spring we headed north to San Francisco and sold our little bunch of cows at a good profit and moved inland toward Sacramento. I told Gem as good as our life was going we were bound to stumble on a pile of gold somewhere.

Gem told me as good as our life was going we didn't need no gold.

She was right, I was wrong we never found any gold.

Lookin back on it, all the gold in the world could not have made two kids any richer than they were.

We worked our way north, earning our keep on various ranches and still buying and selling cattle. The smart ranchers let Gem ride their horses and work their cows. The not so smart ones thought she should be a cook. We didn't last long on those places, there was way more to that girl than being in a kitchen.

It took us close to a year to make it to Sacramento. We stopped on the outskirts and found a cattle buyer and sold him twenty head at what we thought was a remarkable price.

We rolled into town in the Grand Hotel Hamovitz with money in every pocket and decided a night in a fine hotel and a dinner in a fancy restaurant couldn't hurt a thing.

Benny you haven't been there, yet. A fine dinner with a fine woman is one of the true joys of life and we savored it and made it last as long as we could.

Gem and I were standing on the front porch of the restaurant enjoying the night and I guess life in general when a couple of drunk men stumbled out the door and one of them bumped into me by accident. He smiled his best drunk smile and started into apologizing profusely, like drunks everywhere do.

I said I was happy to accept his regrets and started to leave. He grabbed my arm and stopped me.

"I know you?"

"No sir I don't believe you do."

He looked at me with the eyes of a man filled with popskull and dulled senses. He knew what he saw, and he didn't know what he saw, he was trying hard but couldn't' put it all together.

"You sure we have never met?"

"Yes sir, I am."

His drinkin partner said, "leave the kid alone, Tom, we got some business to take care of" and he held up a half full bottle.

The drunk was looking at me and Gem still trying to make the puzzle fit.

Gem took my hand and we walked off the porch toward the hotel. "You know who that was, don't you Davey?"

"Oh boy, I sure do."

"So much for a night in a fancy hotel."

"You think he is still lookin for us?"

"What do you think Davey, of course he is."

"I doubt he knows we are here in California, I mean how in the world could he?"

"That's not an answer I might have at my ready disposal, however that is how he earns his living."

"I wish I was a better shot."

We left that night and headed north and east, at a good clip. Our plan was to be as far as we could be by the time the liquid on and in his brain dissipated and he was able to put thoughts together again. Although we gave a lot of thought to that back shootin bastard and if he was truly on our trail, we weren't particularly scared or worried. We had been schooled on the fine art of disappearance by some of the best bushwhackers that ever taught the course.

A couple of years slipped by and thoughts of the special back shootin deputy faded.

Gem and I had figured out a pretty good life for ourselves here in California. We played the same game, buy a few cows, then sell a few cows and move on.

It was with horses where we began to make good money. Our plan never wavered, I would start the colts and Gem would put the finish on them. That girl had as fine a touch with a horse as any one I have ever seen.

At that time there was a cow outfit called Miller and Lux. It was said that a fellow could ride from San Francisco to Oregon and never leave Miller Lux holdings and ride a Miller Lux horse every step of the way.

At their peak the company ran a million mother cows. A rep from Miller Lux heard about the fine touch Gem could put on a horse and asked us if he could buy the really good ones for his managers to ride? If we would agree he would set us up on a pretty little ranch in Nevada on the outskirts of the Black Rock desert.

We agreed and moved to Nevada. We moved out of the Grand Hotel Hamovitz and moved into a real house. We kept the Hamovitz down by the hay yard, just in case.

Me and a cowboy named Hill, I can't remember if it was Tom or Mike. I think it was Mike maybe Tom, it don't matter. We started the horses in those days when they were around five or six years old. They were big and rough and hard to ride.

Hill, it was Mike I remember now, and I would bring um into this big round pen and start in. Most of the horses we started ended up what were called cowboy horses, meaning they would turn left and right, stop pretty good, not buck too much and tolerate being roped off of. The good ones went to Gem and she made some beautiful straight up spade bit horses.

Some of those horses went to various ranch managers but most of them went to Mr. Miller. Mr. Miller had a standing order when Gem said she was satisfied with a horse it was to go to a certain ranch somewhere or another and Gem and I were to deliver it. He made it clear he would only ride geldings, but every once in a while, Gem would slip in a very well broke mare for him to try.

Mr. Richards face was flushed, and he was sweating. This was getting harder and harder.

"You want to stop for a while?" I asked.

"Ya I do, I really do, none the less I don't think I ought to. Startin up is getting harder and harder."

"You sure? I can wait, I got all the time in the world." The instant the words came out I knew it was not only wrong it was a really, really stupid thing to say.

Mr. Richards gave me one of his looks, the one that asks the question if you think you are smart enough to inhale then exhale on your own. I guess he forgave me, he started back in.

Benny, we had stumbled into a gold mine of a life. Our part in the war was far in the past. Our life of violence and sudden death seemed gone as well. From time to time we encountered former rebel men and former union soldiers. They for the most part wanted no more to be a part of the war than Gem and I did. It was over, regardless of how a person viewed the outcome it was over. Winners or losers we had one thing in common, memories. Christ Ben, I still got them.

Most of the time I can push them to the back of my brain, but sometimes I can't. I hope against all hope this is not something you will have to deal with. You can get past it but pray to God you won't have to.

The memories Gem and I had, with the exception of the deaths of our parents, were the same. They affected us in different ways, naturally. We had each other to get us through and help with the darker nights. Gem was better at it than I was, no matter how bad. Maybe the greatest help we had with getting over the war was Henry Miller. By that I mean he gave us the greatest job in the world. In me and Gems world, anyway.

Mr. Miller sent us up and down and all over the west coast delivering the horses Gem and I got to ride. He saw to it we stayed at the best ranches, got exposed to some of the finest horsemen of the time and always, always had time to talk to us about cows and horses or simply things of interest. He was the one that told us we should be married and put together a wedding for us at his ranch headquarters in Los Banos.

Mr. Richards started to leak out some tears, then he gave up and cried. Benny, she looked beautiful that day, she wore a white wedding dress, Mr. Miller had made for her in San Francisco. Somehow, she had managed to smooth down that wild mop of red curly hair. I loved her red hair, she hated her red hair. I used to tease her about it, saying things like she must have been a wild Irish princess in a past life. Or she was red in the head like a dick of a dog.

Mr. Richards stopped and looked my way with a sly smile. You know endearing things, things a woman loves to hear. "Benny, I have never been so tired, if it is alright with you we can call it a day."

I wanted to say no it was not ok, he didn't give the appearance of a man with many days left.

"Yes, sir tomorrow is a new day, if you want I'll go whistle Dixie and we can look over the horses." He just looked at me.

Chapter XXV

We would not be whistling Dixie tomorrow or any day. It occurred to me I should go get Jake and ride him up to the house for Mr. Richards. I thought he would enjoy that. I did and rode him to the screened in porch.

Maggie yelled at me from the upstairs window. "Get that damned horse off the lawn."

Mr. Richards croaked out, "Atta boy!"

I rode Jake back to the barn with a smile. That was the best I had felt in a while, it was the best anybody had felt in a while. Mr. Richards seemed a little scattered when I went in to check on him the next morning.

"What were we talking about last time, Benny?"

"You and Gem were training horses for Miller Lux."

"Oh ya, that's how we ended up here in Likely."

"How's that?"

"Henry Miller and a couple of his men were making one of his tours around his holdings and spent the night at the ranch where Gem and I lived. The next morning, he told us about this part of the country and made us an offer. We could homestead a place for our own. He would keep supplying horses for us to ride, to help us get a good start. If we so chose, he would pay us for the horses we brought to him with mostly cattle and not much money. Well, really not too much in the way of cattle either. Finally, he added if it all went bad for us and didn't work out, he would buy the homestead from us after we had proved up.

Gem had spent a little over a year and a half on one of our horses, a shiny copper colored gelding. She had told me on several occasions this was one of the best horses she ever rode and intended to keep him. Gem put Mr. Miller's saddle on that horse and said, "Sir, we will go be homesteaders and you need not invest one minutes worth of time thinking you will have to buy us out. Thank you and please take this horse."

"Bull shit, I'll not take a horse without paying, Mrs. Richards."

"Bull shit, you will take this horse." Gem marched right up to him and pointed her finger at his face. She didn't even come up to his chest. He looked down at her, she looked up at him.

While Henry Miller may have been one of the richest and most powerful men on the whole west coast, he stood no chance with this wild haired miniature combination of bushwhacker and Indian fighter wantin to turn homesteader.

Henry Miller was not dumb, he held out his hand and said. "Thank you, ma'am I will take good care of this horse."

As the men rode off I said, "Gem think we should have talked this over, I mean this is a pretty big move in our life?"

"No."

"What do you mean, no?"

"Davey, what is there to talk about? You know this is the way to go, you can see that as clear as I can."

I could see she was right, that didn't take any vast amount of brain power, still I would have liked to have been included in the talks. But really what was the main irritant to me, I liked that horse. We moved back into the Grand Hotel Hamovitz and started in our life in north east California.

The first three or maybe four years were the hardest. This was sagebrush and some trees not much else. The best place for the Hamovitz was down by the creek and naturally that worked best for the garden. We built from there.

The first year Gem and I dug the well and built some of the horse corrals. We day worked when we could for the Williams family and others when we could. Mostly we did pretty much what we had been doing since we left the war, making our living buying and selling livestock.

It didn't take all that long for the word to spread about the fine touch Gem could put on a horse and soon we had more buyers that horses. Not that bad a problem to have, I would say.

The old timers around this part of the country told us later, that first winter we were here was the worst they had seen in years. Benny, they were not sharing some big secret with us.

We lived in the Grand Hotel Hamovitz, a God damned wagon! Everything froze. Except us, we had that little tin stove Gem had bought off the peddler.

Gem was quite cavalier about my apology, like she promised, I didn't have to write it out.

We found and chopped wood every day. We chopped ice for the stock three sometimes four times a day.

Everything we had saved from our little garden froze and was ruined. We lived on jack rabbits and an occasional deer, and ducks, ducks and more ducks.

When the spring finally arrived, Gem told me this was the summer we were going to build a house and we did. It wasn't this one, this one came later, although a lot of the wood in this one came from the original. We managed to get it built and the roof on by fall. Moving in was easy, we didn't have nothin.

We made a trip to Alturas and bought the stove that's in the kitchen. Gem suggested we feed the Hamovitz to the new stove, to make sure we never spent another night in it. I agreed, but we couldn't bring ourselves to do it.

"Mr. Richards is that the Hamovitz you use to mount horses with?"

"Why yes, it is Benny, that wagon has more miles on it than those old gals that work the cribs down in Reno." Mr. Richards coughed a little at his humor that led to more coughing and then to not being able to catch his breath.

We sat and waited and when he stopped I asked, "Feel like carrying on, sir?

"Give me a minute."

"Take all the time you need."

"I don't feel I have all that much, what do you think Ben?"

"Plenty, I think you have plenty of time." I knew he didn't.

The next winter was milder than the last and we had nowhere near the hard times of the preceding winter. Unknown to us Gem had caught that summer and the pregnancy showed up that winter. We bumped around her big belly in that little place and laughed all winter.

In the spring Gem foaled the prettiest little baby girl you ever saw. She had fine blond hair and blue eyes, she was the spitting image of Gem. We named her Felicity. She lived two months. She never made a sound that day, she died looking at us. One instant she was here and the next she wasn't. Gem took it better than I did.

We took out our grief on the horses, I got rougher for a while, and Gem got gentler.

Mr. Richards sort of waved his arms around as best he could, in frustration. "You just go on Benny, that's all you can do. Feelin sorry for yourself don't get you nothin, you just go on." That is what we did.

We built up our cow numbers, we took on a few more horses and we started in building this house. It worked, we got past it and found our place again.

The next time she was with child, we got William Clark and we had eighteen almost nineteen years of pure joy.

"Benny no more today, I need to think about some of this. Will you help Maggie move the rest of the house and in a couple of days help her move me?" He wasn't going to make the move, and we both knew it.

"No problem as much as you weigh I can carry you to the new place, we won't need the truck."

"Put it in your ass, kid." He laughed until he coughed, and he was still coughing when I left.

My dad called that evening and asked how Mr. Richards was holding up and were we about moved out. "Dad, I don't think Mr. Richards will make the move."

"What do you mean, make the move? Won't or can't? We have to do something Ben. Rudy and his family are ready to move in and start running the ranch and it's time for you to be back here for school."

"Dad I don't think it will be all that long, can you give me and Mr. Richards a little more time?" I felt like if I gave in I would be crying and slobbering to my dad and I wanted to do just that, but I knew that was the last thing I could do, those days were gone.

"I don't know son, as much as we want it to the world doesn't often move at the speed we need it to."

I did start crying then. Not so much as I was sad, I was sad. It was more than that, I was mad pure unadulterated pissed off. The God damned world was going to move at the speed I wanted.

"No dad, this time the world will turn as I see fit!"

"I don't know Benny, there are things going on here that can't be changed."

"Bullshit!"

"Benny you listen to me."

"No dad you listen to me, I will not move that old man. I mean to let him die in his own house."

"Ben."

"No." The phone got quiet. "I got to go dad, I know you can understand and make it all work. This is how it has to be." I hung up without waiting for his answer. He didn't call back.

The next morning, I went to check on him, the pillow he was leaning on was all that was holding him up, to say he looked bad would be a complement.

"I heard you on the phone with your father last night, don't get cross ways with him on my account. That wouldn't be right."

"How much did you hear?"

"Not a lot really, but enough."

"I once knew a guy that was so smart he could walk up to a hole in the ground and tell you exactly how long it took to dig, how much dirt came out of it, how much the dirt weighed and then fall in the hole. I guess that's where I am now, in the bottom of that hole. You ain't movin until you say the word."

Mr. Richards laughed and coughed, and his eyes got moist. "Benny you remind me of my boy William Clark at your age, he was as hard headed as you are, in fact I used to call him Billy marble head."

"I will take that as complementary."

"Don't."

But, of course I did.

Chapter XXVI

W e did good here. Slowly but surely, we built up our cow herd. Any year we were profitable we bought more land and built up the ranch.

Gems reputation as a horse hand and trainer spread out and people from all over wanted to buy horses from us. I say us because about half the dumb sons a bitches wouldn't believe a woman could make so fine a horse. We let them think what they wanted and spent their money, just the same.

I will tell you the ones that showed doubt paid more for the privilege of being well mounted. The years went by, life got settled. Thoughts of the war became less and less, until they were mostly gone.

I was at the feed store when a group of the county's leading citizens cornered me and asked what my thoughts might be on running for county commissioner.

I thanked them profusely and said I sure would give it some thought, but that I needed to talk it over with my wife.

The first impression we had was what a hoot, me in politics. At first, we laughed at the very idea.

Gem was the first to mention although quite a few years had gone by, we were still former border ruffians and the much written about notorious Lawrence assassins.

To which I replied, "I don't know Gem, I seriously doubt anyone around here has any idea of all that."

"I wish you wouldn't."

As usual Gem was right. I ran against a sheep man from the north end of the valley and got trounced. I was for a water plan to irrigate the valley and he was against it.

We both campaigned hard. We talked to the people, to the newspapers, to just about anyone who cared to listen. In the end his message was better, and he went to Sacramento and I stayed home.

Truth be known I came to know and like him, he did a good job representing our county. After dipping my toe in the political world briefly and with results that could be called less than over whelming, I abandoned all that nonsense and went back to ranching.

The next few years' word spread out of this area on the kind of horses Gem turned out and we prospered. People came from all over to look and buy horses.

I still rode colts although not as much. I became more of a horse trader, a damned salesman and I loved it. Sellin things is the ultimate competition, they know what they want, and you know what you want. It is naturally more fun when you win the deal, than the other way around. Either way it will get the heart pumping.

I saw this fellow riding up the road, it was a beautiful fall day the leaves had changed colors but hadn't started to fall yet. He rode right up to the house and called out, "Hello the house, any one in there?" He sounded pleasant enough.

I walked up from the barn sort of getting into salesman mode and thinking about what horse might be of interest to him. As I got closer I could see he sat his horse in a kind of odd way.

He turned his horse toward me. I saw his withered arm.

I knew exactly who he was.

"Your name David Richards?"

"Yes."

"I saw your name in the paper, you ran for public office."

"Yes."

Maybe it's not him, maybe he doesn't recognize me, and maybe he just wants to buy a horse. He reached in his jacket pocket and pulled out what looked to be some sort of stiff paper.

He tossed it on the ground by my feet. It was an old tin type of a couple of kids.

"How could a filthy no good secesh bastard like you have the unmitigated gall to not only show his face in the daylight, but run for government office?"

I bent over and picked up the picture and when I looked up I was looking at the barrel of his revolver.

"It took me awhile to figure out that little red headed girl was the other half of the Lawrence assassins. I should have my way with her when I had the chance."

"I don't recall you ever having that chance, in fact all I recall is you ruining a perfectly good coffee pot with your head."

"Where is she, by God I'll have my due now, that little whelp owes me!"

"I wonder do you think of me every time you try to scratch your ass with that bum arm you are carrying around, there slick."

"Laugh all you want the both of you are going back to Kansas in a pine box."

I heard two sounds at the exact same time. I heard him cock his pistol. I heard this wild primal sound, that was a combination rebel yell with some Comanche war cry and wild Irish princess all combined into one. Gem came off the roof of the porch on a dead run with that wild red hair of hers on full display and waving my father's sword above her head. She looked like, I don't know what she looked like, something out of the Arabian Knights or Joan of Arc or maybe the Crusades. Whatever she looked like, it worked. I froze in place and looked up.

The red leg son of a bitch and would be righter of wrongs, was so startled by Gems antics he dropped his pistol and looked up, too. Even his horse was just as boogered as we were. He managed to use his good arm to grab at the reins as his horse reared up in fright. The only thing he succeeded in doing, however, was to pull the horse over on top of him.

Gem missed him altogether and landed on her butt, she was not even close. The horse ran off a ways.

I picked up the pistol and then picked up Gem. "You ok?"

"I think so, ya I'm fine." She kinda patted herself. "How you suppose he's doin?" We both heard this little pitiful whimper.

"You gotta help me I can't feel my legs." Then a little louder. "Get over here." We walked over to him, laying there on the ground.

I looked him straight in the eye and put the barrel of his pistol to his chest.

"Davey wait!" Gem put her hand on top of mine, it was warm. She gave her head just the slightest of a nod. I pulled the trigger.

Gem didn't say anything, I didn't say anything for the longest time. Then Gem hugged me and softly said. "He should have stuck to back shootin, he was better at that." Gem walked over and picked up the tin type and looked at me.

"Is that us Davey?"

"Yes, it is."

"I remember that hat, Felicity gave it to me." We left Fort Smith in a hurry as I recall and didn't make it back to the photographer to pick it up."

"How did he end up with it?"

"I don't know, I don't care. What I do know is that bastard brought back the war to me and with it all the memories of how much it cost me and you."

"I'm pretty sure it is over now." Gem looked at me, like only Gem could look at me.

"Davey let me ask you this question." A big Gem smile followed. "You ever in your life see two cuter kids than these two?"

After a while we took him up to the big tree and buried him.

A few days later I turned his horse loose on the smoke creek desert to run with the wild horses. She was a good lookin mare, no sense in letting her go to waste.

Mr. Richards stopped talking and looked out toward the yard. "Benny you tell me, was I right or was I wrong killin that man?"

"Sir, I don't think you really want my opinion, I think you and Gem worked out the right or wrong of it a long time ago."

Mr. Richards smiled at me and said, "Ben, I believe you to be a good man and I believe you know when to speak and when to shut up."

I reached out and took a hold of his hand, it seemed like the right thing to do.

"Ben my string has just about run out and I'm going to have to tell that story again pretty quick now, I think." He closed his eyes and said real soft, "I sure hope God is as understanding as you are Benny."

I left and went in the kitchen with Maggie. She was crying hard.

"Is the end Benny?"

God damn how would I know? "No, I think there might be a little more he wants to tell us, I hope." There was, it wasn't much.

Later that afternoon I stopped by the porch to check on him, it took all his effort to hold up his hand and beckon to me.

"Nobody ever said anything to us about that day and you know Gem and I spoke to no one. We went on with life and it was mostly good, like I say. William Clark grew up straight and tall and was by far the best man with a rope I ever saw. He just had to go to Cuba and do his part, be a hero. He died of dysentery on a filthy cot and was buried somewhere in the jungle, in a mass grave. I can't tell you I ever really healed up from that loss. Gem and my life was filled with loss from the time we were children.

We moved on again and again or at least we tried to. Gem died as a result of the influenza epidemic in 1918. The word was Germany had started it because they lost the war. I can't say it mattered much. She was just as dead. One day she was fine, the next day she had a fever, the next day she got so hot her hair fell out and the next day she was gone.

Benny, you might think because I had lived with and around death my whole life, I would be better prepared, I wasn't. The loss from death is unavoidable, we all know that. The worst of it though is something no one thinks too much about. The older you get the less people around you knew the person that died, like you did.

Gem and I always, always had each other to talk it over. We would laugh at the funny parts, be sad at the others. Sometimes something would be going on that would jog an old memory. Whether you laughed or cried or got disgusted it didn't matter, it helps in your life to share things about the dead and in that way, in your mind at least, you keep them around. I got drunk and stayed there for years, wishin I could die. Wishin it would have been me not Gem.

I didn't die instead I let our ranch go to hell, I sold off our cows, the horse program went in the toilet and I went in the toilet with everything else. Alcohol is a funny thing, after a while I didn't want to die anymore, and I didn't want to live either, I just wanted to wallow in my self-pity. Woe is me, woe is me. Jesus Christ, woe is me!

I got in a fight in the bar one night with a hay farmer from over on the Nevada border and when the cops showed up I got arrested and hauled to jail. The judge was a lodge brother and a good friend, he made me stay in that cell for a month to dry out.

When he let me out he told me in his opinion I was too good a man to give it all over to booze and if he heard even a weak rumor I was in some bar somewhere he was going to put me back in that jail cell.

I made my promise and walked out meanin to keep it and instead turned toward the bar, I needed just one drink, bad. I almost made it. A little fat Indian woman ran smack dab into me and about knocked me over.

"Cowboy you look like you could use a good meal, if you got some place for me to cook it, I'm your gal.

Maggie Pete came into my life that afternoon. I am not a highly religious man, Benny. The death of my father that day in Missouri took most of that from me. I do, however, believe there was some sort of divine intervention going on that day. I know that as sure as I know the sun comes up in the east.

She couldn't replace Gem. I didn't want her to and she didn't want to. Maggie Pete is a force of nature and I'm better for her and because of her. I will miss her.

Benny, I need some rest now, come around and see me in the morning and we can tell each other about all the good horses we have known and rode."

His light went out that night with his gift of divine intervention, sitting right there beside him.

The funeral was big, people came from all over. Maggie had asked if after the service, would it, could it be alright for everyone to come to the ranch? "Davey would like that."

Mr. Richards lodge brothers brought tables and chairs from the lodge. Women brought their specialty foods and filled the tables to their full capacity. There must have been twenty variations of potato salad.

Even though there was no furniture or anything else that showed Mr. Richards ever lived there, it was a perfect send off.

Men toasted Davey Richards and told funny stories about him and the ranch. Women hovered around Maggie, as only women that care can do. No one, that I heard, made any mention of the shooting all those years ago. I suppose I was the only one that truly knew the story and it was not my place to share it.

I saw Jeanie, she came over and hugged me and did her best to drag me into a conversation, but my heart wasn't in it and I left her and walked out to the front porch. My dad followed me out and put his arm around my shoulder and started to tell me about how many people had come up to him and told him what a good man I was becoming and that he could not be more proud of me.

I would be a liar if I told you his arm on my shoulder didn't feel good. I wanted to cry, but instead I said, "Dad I want you to look up and in your mind I want you to picture a woman with wild red hair running off this roof with a combination rebel yell and Comanche war cry, waving a sword over her head that had last seen action in the Crimean War, in defense of her man."

He didn't say a word, he just looked at me. It seemed a long time ago when my mother said a boy needs to have an old man in his life. I cried then.

Epilogue
1945

My parents picked me up from the dock, I wasn't really out of the Navy yet. I got a two week pass and we headed to the ranch.

Mom made me kind of nervous, she would not stop turning around to look at me. Dad did his best to keep the conversion going and light. We talked cow prices, of course, actually I liked that. Dad told me in his best salesman's voice he had a new set of colts that had showed promise and when I was ready so were they. He caught my eye and looked at me in the rear-view mirror.

"The old Richards place is empty." I didn't know how to answer him, so I didn't. "With the war going on good cowboys became hard to find." I was still at a loss for words. "What I am quite poorly trying to tell you is, I would like you to run it."

"Thank you, Dad, for the vote of confidence. I mean that. If it is alright with you, I need to think it over. At this time, I can't tell you the cowboy life is for me. I have been giving a lot of thought of moving to Reno and going to college. I think I would like to be a writer."

He started to say something, stopped and looked at me in the mirror again. "You always were a hard-headed little shit. That's what I like about you. Anything I can do to help, let me know, son."

Neither one of them made any more mention of the war, except to express joy it was over. I fell asleep in the back seat and before long we were driving up the road to the ranch. My sisters bolted out of the house and threw their arms around me, just about taking us all to the ground. They cried tears of joy and must have told me how glad they were I was home at least twelve million times.

From around the side of the house Joaquin walked over, shook my hand and smiled. "You see the elephant?"

Ever since there have been army's battling each other, the survivors have always had sayings like that. Maybe it shows you understand, you have war in common, I don't know, but mostly I think that is the way to talk about it without talking about it.

"I saw that son of a bitch." No one standing there had the slightest idea what we were talking about. Joaquin and I did, we knew, and worse yet we knew the elephant would always be there, somewhere.

Dinner that night was fun, it was like old times, except my mother still kept looking at me.

Finally, I said, "Mom stop staring at me, I'm back, it's over. No one can hurt me now."

She didn't stop, she got better, but didn't stop. I figured that would take a while. Toward the end of dinner, it hit me just how tired I was. I guess my mother knew.

"I made up your old room, Benny. It's all ready for you."

"Thanks mom. I'm ready for it." No one had called me Benny in four years. It felt good; it felt right. I had thought and wondered if I was ever going to sleep in my own bed ever again.

Once on some uncharted, unnamed atoll in the south pacific, I was pretty convinced I wasn't.

"By the way I forgot to tell you a package showed up for you a while back, it is on your bed."

The package was a box, it was long, narrow, and wrapped in brown butcher paper and tied up with string. The address was printed in neat small hand writing. I knew instantly what was in the box.

"Into the valley of death rode the six hundred."

About the Author

DENNIS HILL worked on the mountain in Sun Valley, Idaho, packed mules and was a big game guide in Montana. He wrote his first book, *I Never Got to Meet Joe Back* based on his time as a guide. Hill grew up in Nevada, rode bucking horses (poorly), spent some time wandering around Europe and even helped build atomic bombs at the test site outside of Las Vegas.

After finishing his first book, he wrote **Out in the Sagebrush**, "A good cowboy yarn". **Gem: An American Story,** was the result of research of the conflict between Missouri and Kansas and his desire to continue storytelling, something he enjoys doing from his home in Reno, Nevada with his wife, Margaret, on a little place with horses, cows and border collies.